FOR THE ONE
A COLLECTION OF SHORT STORIES

STEVE WALSH

This book is a work of fiction. Names, characters, places, churches, denominations, corporations and incidents are entirely the product of the author's imagination and are used fictitiously. Any resemblance to actual events, locals, or persons, living or dead is unintended and entirely coincidental.

No part of this publication may be reproduced, distributed, or transmitted in any form or by any means, including photocopying, recording or other electronic or mechanical methods, without the prior written permission of the publisher, except in the case of brief quotations embodied in critical reviews and certain other noncommercial uses permitted by copyright law.

In accordance with the U.S. Copyright Act of 1976, the scanning, up-loading, and electronic sharing of any part of this book without the permission of the publisher is unlawful piracy and theft of the author's intellectual property. If you would like to use material from this book (other than for review purposes), prior written permission must be obtained by contacting the publisher. Thank you for your support of the author's rights.

Scripture quotations from The World English Bible.

First eBook and printed edition - 2025

ISBN: 978-1-7334336-5-5 (Softcover)

ISBN: 978-1-7334336-6-2 (E Book)

Copyright © 2025 by Steve Walsh - All rights reserved.
www.evangelions.org

All opinions, theological positions
and other mistakes belong to the author.

Also by Steve Walsh

Growing Older with God

The Redemption of George

While Good Men Slept

I
THE GOD FACTOR

Joan Dodson was the high priestess of prediction. Her mother claimed the gift came from her grandfather. Her father said the gift came from his uncle. Each wanted to claim a hand in her extraordinary ability to predict the outcomes of certain key factors.

She was a celebrated guest of the White House and many alphabet agencies who hoped to recruit her talents. She appeared on all the celebrity talk shows where she performed simple prophetic outcomes. Try as they might she never revealed the secret to winning the Lotto, Vegas or the Stock Market. She kept that information to herself and her offshore bank accounts.

This morning as in every morning she stood before five elevator doors on the thirtieth floor of her high-rise apartment. Tapping her bottom lip with a manicured index finger she mentally calculated the probability of which elevator would open first after she pressed the lighted down arrow.

She knew that each of the five cars was moving up from the lobby at a speed of six meters per second. She also knew the number of persons each car might hold and the number of stops it might make. She computed the odds that one or more cars were out of service. She factored the possibility that firefighters below had commandeered a car for emergency use. She considered the possibility that a power glitch had damaged the elevator's internal computer. There was the remote possibility that seismic activity had twisted the elevator shafts forcing the cars to slow down. Of course there hadn't been any seismic activity in Abundance Falls since 1884 but the possibility still had to be considered.

She then pondered the possibility that a gaggle of apartment dwellers had crowded into a car below triggering its load sensors causing it to automatically bypass its routine stops. She then considered the prospect that a disabled person might have slowed things down. She finally estimated the odds of a delivery driver having blocked an elevator's doors while making a delivery. There were literally millions of different floor stop combinations that the cars could make on their way to her floor. Yet she played this game without fail every day for her own amusement.

Tick tock, tick tock. Which of the five cars would arrive when she pushed the lighted down arrow? *I predict car number three will be first to open it's doors, "in... five... four... three...two...one..."*

She pointed at three's door like a magician ordering an assistant to open a curtain.

"...now."

Door number three opened obediently.

Damn, I'm good!"

She hadn't missed a prediction in months.

STEPPING inside the elevator she paused to admire her reflection in its mirrored covered walls. Cosmetic surgeries had reshaped her once horsey face into an almost attractive woman. She wore large Jackie O sunglasses with big circular earrings. A wide gold bracelet gripped her wrist as a reminder of her success.

It was bitterly cold outside so she wore a silver fox Ushanka hat, a shimmering red puffer jacket and a pair of black skinny jeans with shearling lined mid-calf boots. She twisted around to get a good look at her perky bottom. *Pretty good for a scrawny girl from Nowheresville,* she thought. Pooching her lips she blew her reflection a kiss.

The sound of a ship's bell announced an incoming text message. She began tapping the phone's screen like a chicken pecking for grain. "Wrong you f'kin numb-nuts, the risk factor is 1.78 percent, not 1.87 percent."

She rolled her eyes in exasperation, took a breath and hitched up her shoulder bag. She decided it might be a good time to send her sister Megan a message before she lost reception.

Had a great Thanksgiving, she texted.

A lie.

She made the annual trek more out of obligation than desire. It was always painful. Three nights sleeping on a fold out bed, days spent enduring Megan's husband shouting at his football teams on TV and evenings being forced to eat Megan's culinary concoctions cooked with slabs of lard, sticks of butter and fried in buckets of oil. Joan felt like she needed to bring her own defibrillator.

But the real reason she hated the visit was because Megan had gone from being a fun-loving sister to an intolerant religious fanatic. It happened right after Pastor Thad Wilkes scared Megan into thinking she was some kind of monster damned forever to hell.

"You're a loathsome sinner, a worthless insect in the eyes of a wrathful God who seeks your damnation!" he yelled, from the pulpit.

Megan fell to her knees right into the clutches of Pastor Wilkes where she sobbed deep sighs of remorse and sought forgiveness. But but there was non forthcoming, only more calls for more repentance and shame.

From that moment Megan was obsessed with how people needed to get right with God, what people did in the privacy of their bedroom and what to expect at the second coming. Eventually Megan met her husband Doug at a church gathering, tied the knot, had twins, got a job at the Water Company, fattened up and turned into a fundamentalist prig.

Things got worse between the sisters after Megan

became more outspoken against lesbianism, abortion and declared that Godly woman shouldn't go to the vanity parlor, which is what she called the beauty salon.

Every Thanksgiving for the past ten years Joan received the same lecture on the sins of wearing jewelry and expensive clothing. Joan shrugged it off. If these were sins against God then she was happy to be on the express train to hell.

Try as she might Joan could never reason with Megan. Eventually she gave up trying. She pitied her sister for believing Pastor Wilkes' religious nonsense. It wasn't that Joan didn't believe in a higher power it's just that she didn't think that a higher power had such absurd rules.

Joan considered herself a spiritual person in touch with her chakras, a holistic Divinity and a pantheon of angelic beings. As a spiritual person she cherished the sight of the Abundance Falls skyline from the rooftop of her condo. She loved the sacred feeling her building's indoor swimming pool, spa, gym and personal trainer gave her. Then there was her heavenly Aston Martin in powder blue (to match the color of her eyes) what provided a sense of divine freedom. This morning she wouldn't need it because a private limousine was picking her up.

Joan smiled and momentarily reflected on how her life had dramatically changed since she'd been named the first female President and Chief Actuary of the Transoceanic Insurance Corporation, the largest maritime underwriter in the world.

A PLEASANT TONE chimed and the twin elevator doors whooshed opened. In moments she stepped into the condo's opulent lobby.

"You look absolutely fetching, mum," the concierge greeted her in a smooth British accent. "Your limousine is waiting."

"Morning Edward," she muttered, without looking up from her cell phone.

"Mind your step, mum. We had a icy bluster last night and it's a bit slippery outside."

She nodded and held up her phone speaking into it like it was a dictation machine. "The probability of error is 7.62 of the design coefficient, not 6.87 as you've calculated. Let's get this right team."

"Of course, mum." Edward stammered, not knowing if he was speaking to him. He quickly pushed open the building's glass entrance and stepped smoothly to the limo where he gracefully opened the rear door allowing Joan to slide in.

"Your bags are already loaded, mum. Will there be anything else?"

She barely noticed him until she suddenly blurted. "No wait, yes - I almost forgot Munchkin. Would you run up and get her?"

Munchkin was her beloved comfort cat she'd paid $25,000. dollars for. She never went anywhere without her.

"Already done mum."

Edward nodded to an assistant standing nearby who ran to the other side of the limo and placed a small pet carrier in the back seat.

"Edward you're such a dear," she replied. "How can I ever thank you?"

She reached into her purse for a tip.

"No need mum. My reward is to serve you."

Naturally, she thought.

Edward bowed his head and pinched the brim of his topper. Without a word she raised the tinted glass of the car's electric window leaving him to smile at his own reflection.

"Be careful my young friend," he said, under his breath, "They say that you get what you give." He watched the limo speed off creating small snow flurries in its wake.

JOAN LEANED BACK and cradled herself in the vehicle's soft leather seat. She scrolled through her emails. After a few minutes she opened the pet carrier and brought Munchkin to her chest.

"Mummy almost forgot her widdle baby," she cooed, stroking its spotted coat. She held it up to the window. "Look at all those sad little losers crunching through the dirty snow on their way to work. That could have been me but mommy has a gift and I'm going to milk it for all it's worth."

Munchkin purred happily.

Joan was on her way to inspect Peter Wendigo's latest ship under construction. He'd personally selected her to evaluate all possible insurance risks that his three billion dollar submarine presented.

Peter, along with the rest of the maritime industry respected Joan's astonishing grasp of mathematics, insurance algorithms and her comprehension of the factors that governed random chance. To put it mildly she was considered a probabilistic and actuarial genius.

Joan's ability to mentally dissect a ship's design, construction, materials and potential uses and then accurately predict the probability of accidents, incidents, structural failures and calamities resulting in unforeseen litigation or liability claims had saved her clients billions of dollars. Industry leaders called her 'Joan of Ark' and she was a revered goddess in the pantheon of modern establishment feminism.

The privacy screen separating her from the driver lowered. "Ms. Dodson I am Hector Abadi. I am instructed to drive you to Mr. Wendigo's private jet." He spoke over his shoulder in broken English. "This is agreeable?"

Joan looked at his picture on the chauffeur's license clipped to the visor above his head.

Hector chuckled. "I know what you think Ms. Dodson. Crazy name, yes? My father is Christian from Syria, my mother a Jew from Spain. Very unusual, yes?"

What are the odds? she smiled to herself. Then switching topics she asked him, "Are you a betting man?"

Hector looked at her warily in the rear view mirror.

"Don't worry, I won't get you into any trouble. As a matter of fact you might come out a hundred dollars richer."

"I am listening with both my ears," he replied.

"How long have you been driving Hector?"

"For this company, eight years. Before that I drive for His Royal Highness Mohammed bin Abdul ten years."

She paused and mentally calculated the impact of traffic at this hour, the chances of a mechanical breakdown, the timing of traffic lights, the effect of ice on the road, the probability of encountering a police car. Then she calculated the experience of the driver and what she called the G factor, which accounted for the unknown. Satisfied with her analysis she pulled a hundred-dollar bill from her purse and held it up.

"I will give you a hundred dollars if you can get me to the terminal in less than thirty minutes."

Hector's eyes widen as he looked into the rearview mirror. He shifted the toothpick in his mouth from one side to the other. "Normally takes more than an hour this time of day."

"I know," Joan nodded.

"And what if I cannot?" he asked, through his toothpick.

"You'll owe me a penny," she explained. "I just want to see if you can do it. Don't worry I'm betting you can." Actually she was betting on her own skills of prediction.

Hector was silent for a few moments.

"Okay, I know few tricks. With God's blessing we will do it — Inshallah."

The privacy screen buzzed up and Hector immediately executed a sharp right hand turn, stepped hard on the accelerator and raced down a deserted alley. Joan started the countdown timer on her Patek Philippe chronograph.

God willing, Joan thought. Sounds like something my

crazy sister would say. *What was up with these religious nuts? God had nothing to do with it. Random chance, probability and some human ingenuity was what it had to do with.* She rubbed a porthole in the foggy window and peered out at the freezing pedestrians battling the bitter cold on the streets.

Hector threaded his way through the city in a pattern of wild zigs and daring zags until he abruptly made a sharp left hand turn, sped up, blew through a series of yellow cones, turned right again and proudly announced, "Ms. Dodson we are here and early I think!"

The limo skidded across a couple of feet of ice to a halt. Joan looked at her watch and praised herself.

Exactly as I calculated, she thought. *I am so damned good.*

"Well done Hector," she said handing him a crisp hundred dollar bill."

"Placing one hand over his heart he said, "May Allah protect you."

SHE DIDN'T HEAR HIM. She was already moving toward Peter's private Gulfstream where an elegant woman wearing a full-length fur trimmed coat with matching fur hat stood waiting for her at the bottom of the staircase. She opened her arms in welcome. "Good morning Ms. Dodson. My name is Sarah, I'll be serving you today."

The woman's voice murmured like a tranquil brook. Long reddish hair fell gracefully across her powerful shoulders framing a softly sculpted face that looked vaguely Asian. Two coal black eyes regarded Joan with such penetrating intensity that it made Joan feel guilty, like she should bow down and worship. Joan was mesmerized. She struggled to keep herself from outright gawking.

"We're waiting for a few more guests," Sarah said, gesturing to the open cabin door with an upturned palm.

Joan thought that the jet had been reserved exclusively for her but she obeyed without comment. *Who cares so long as Peter's six-figure check cashes?*

A moment later she sank into an over stuffed leather chair next to a window. She was the only passenger in the plush cabin. Two pilots sat in the cockpit conducting their preflight checklist. Compulsively she checked her smart phone.

"This plane have Wi-Fi?"

"Of course Ms. Dodson. The password is: *repent* in lower case.

Before she could key in the word a voice said, "Excuse me, I believe we'll be traveling together."

A small handsome man with the suntanned look of a seasoned traveller stood next to her. He was meticulously dressed, wearing a black wool topcoat, a charcoal grey suit, a crisp white cotton shirt and a straw Panama hat. His hair, skin and fingernails were precisely groomed as if he spent time at a salon.

He pointed at the seat facing her. "Do you mind, I thought we might pass the time together." Then he hesitated. "Naturally if you'd rather be alone I'd understand."

Oh great, trapped, she thought. "Sure, that's fine." She nodded towards the seat and returned to her smartphone.

He placed a polished leather briefcase down on the lacquered table separating them. She recognized the brand. *A thousand dollars at least,* she thought.

"I hope we have a safe journey," he said, shrugging off his topcoat to Sarah.

"Don't worry this is one of the safest jets made," Joan muttered. "Statically the odds are in our favor." She hoped the conversation would end.

"My name is David Barlow," he smiled, extending a slender hand. "Do you like statistics?"

"I do," Joan said, brightening. "I use them a lot in my work."

"Let me guess," he said, placing a finger along side his nose. "You're a statistician?"

"No."

"A teacher?"

"Nope"

"An accountant."

"Never."

"A prognosticator?"

Her eyes widened. "Why would you guess that?"

David grinned, "Because I'm an good friend with Peter Wendigo and he told me all about you."

The ice was broken and Joan felt better about the next eight hours in the air.

Their social connection was broken by the clattering entrance of two men and a mule faced woman who stumbled into the cabin thrusting their coats at Sarah and plopping down on their seats.

"Welcome aboard," Sarah said, graciously. She looked at her clipboard. "You would be Mr. Black, Mr. Brown and Ms. Primly?"

"That would be correct," Ms. Primly answered.

"Would you care for a refreshment?"

"Gimme a tall Negroni," Mr. Black ordered. "Heavy on the Negro." He chuckled at his little joke. No one joined him.

"Ignore my friend," Ms. Primly said, rolling her eyes. He doesn't get out much. You can fix me a Cosmopolitan."

Sarah jotted a note and turned to Joan. "And you Ms. Dobson?"

Before she could answer Mr. Brown interrupted brusquely. "I want a Vesper martini, shaken not stirred." His voice tried to imitate the Scottish accent of Sean Connery.

Sarah eyed him evenly. "Certainly sir, I'll make it for your eyes only."

His face broke into the giddy look of a smitten fanboy. "Glad to meet another Bond fan."

THE PILOT'S VOICE INTERRUPTED. "Folks, we've been given clearance for takeoff. Please make sure your seatbelts are fastened."

"This is the best part," David said, excitedly.

The pilot taxied to the main runway where he executed a sharp ninety-degree turn and pointed the aircraft's nose straight down the airstrip. Joan nervously fingered the small cross at her neck.

"So tell me, what are the odds of us crashing?" David asked. Joan eyed him for a moment. *Was he serious?*

He shrugged with his palms upward. "You're the probabilistic genius aren't you?"

She considered the question. "OK. Depends on whether you're speaking about crashing due to pilot error, mechanical problems, weather impact, sabotage or other things like a bird strike or runway obstruction. I think we can rule out sabotage, weather issues and runway obstructions."

David visualized the mental wheels spinning in her head.

"Overall, I'd say the odds are about twenty-nine million to one that we'll crash on take off."

David nodded thoughtfully and looked out of the window, "I can live with that."

But Joan couldn't. Flying terrified her no matter what the odds. She pursed her lips, reached into her purse and found some sedatives she kept for such occasions. She gulped the pills then swallowed them with the booze. She'd have another drink after they took off.

She sank deeper into her seat. She wondered why she couldn't overcome her fear of flying. Millions of people flew every day, nothing happened to them. She felt like a loser needing booze and drugs to fly. It was humiliating. She was a recognized genius in her field and leader of the international woman's movement. Yet she couldn't overcome the terror that came with flying. She hated flying. Flying made her anxious no matter what the odds. She tried calming herself with meditation techniques she learned in Thailand. She removed her boots, sat cross-legged on the seat, closed her eyes and tried to think of pleasant soothing thoughts.

The pilot spooled the engines up, released the brakes and the jet began roaring down the runway

"I love it!" David shouted, his face pressed against the window.

Joan didn't. She squeezed her eyes tightly shut. Yet as hard as she tried she couldn't think of any pleasant or soothing thoughts, just ones of crashing and burning and horrible disfigurement.

As the jet accelerated she felt her body being driven back into the seat and her blood pressure going up. It seemed like forever before she heard the clunk of the wheels clearing the runway and the high pitch whine of the landing gear retracting into the wheel wells. She relaxed her taut muscles, took a measured breath, unfolded her legs and opened her eyes slowly.

"What a marvel of human ingenuity," David said, seemingly unaware of Joan's discomfort. "Can you imagine the technology needed to lift a machine weighing over a hundred thousand pounds to an altitude of fifty thousand feet and then cruising along at .935 Mach, unbelievable!"

Can you imagine shutting your pie hole for five minutes?

"I take it that you like airplanes?" she said. It was more of a statement than question.

"I love flying," he responded. His voice had the excitement of a young boy. "As Leonardo de Vinci once said, 'When you have tasted flight, you will forever walk the earth with your eyes turned skyward.'"

Joan's thoughts were less romantic. "And as Billy Bob Thornton once said, 'I don't have a fear of flying, I have a fear of crashing.'"

THE PLANE BANKED SHARPLY over the river cutting the city into two social worlds. Joan watched the tops of the skyscrapers shrink into pinpoints as the jet gained altitude. David opened his briefcase, Sarah busied herself in the galley, the three bureaucrats ordered more drinks and the pilots fussed about in the cockpit.

Joan turned to Ms. Primly. "Are you three friends?"

"Heavens no," the woman chuckled. "We work at the Department of Diversity. Our job is to insure that Peter hires contractors who meet our expectations."

"Why would he need your permission?"

Ms. Primly huffed as if she wasn't used to answering questions.

"I mean, have you ever built a ship?"

"Shipbuilding has nothing to do with our job."

"Then how can you presume to pick the best candidates to build a ship if you've never been a sailor, marine architect or a builder?"

Ms. Primly's face flushed. "We're not looking for the best candidates we're looking for the right candidates. We've been sent by the Administration to ensure its diversity policies are strictly adhered to."

"Peter's ship isn't being built in the U.S., you have no authority in Israel."

"We have authority everywhere," Ms. Primly snapped. Then she broke into a smarmy smile showing a row of yellowed teeth. "Sweetie, we don't care where someone builds their boat. We can tie them up with enough paperwork to sink the project if we don't like what we see. Besides once it's launched it falls under the world-wide jurisdiction of the United States Government on the high seas."

"The Government doesn't have authority over all the high seas."

Mr. Brown chortled. "We have authority over the entire world. Nobody dares oppose us. What's Peter going to do when one of our destroyers pulls up in the middle of the ocean and demands to inspect his ship?"

"Absolutely nothing," Ms. Primly smirked. The she downed her drink and winked at Joan as if to say, 'check mate.'

She motioned with her glass to Sarah. "Bring me another."

TIME PASSED. Joan yawned, stretched, scratched and toyed with the cross hanging from her neck. Her mind drifted. She thought about the Thanksgiving visit to her sister's house. She wondered why Megan was always so grateful at Thanksgiving. The pitiful woman lived in a shabby town, in a rundown neighborhood, had no savings, no social importance and no future beyond tomorrow.

It was baffling how anyone could live such a dull life and still be so content. The more she thought about it the more annoyed she became thinking about how Megan could have done so much more with her life than having kids and cleaning house.

Yet sometimes when she was alone with a carafe of wine Joan wondered why with all of her wealth, her achievements and her personal freedom she could never shake the feeling that something was missing.

What good was the money if she was too busy to enjoy it? Why have a luxury condo if she was never at home? Why own a prestigious car if she rarely drove it? Why take vacations if they always turned into guilt trips? And what good was independence if there was no one to be free from? The shadow of uncertainty always seemed to follow her.

She leaned her head against the window and watched the frozen landscape pass below until she dozed off.

When Joan opened her eyes David was standing in the galley chatting with Sarah. The three bureaucrats were fast asleep. Mr. Black's chin touched his chest, Mr. Brown's mouth was agape and Ms. Primly snored lightly.

"Not much longer now," David said, returning to his seat.

"How long did I sleep?"

"Most of the trip, we're passing by the island of Cyprus right now."

She looked out the window at the blue Mediterranean. "Wow, I was really out."

"Like the dead," he replied. "Say, I noticed the cross around your neck."

"Oh, it's nothing," she replied, with an air of indifference. "It's just a sentimental gift from my sister."

"So you're a Christian?"

"I guess you could say so, I was raised one." She wondered what was on his mind.

"Do you still go to church?"

"I'm technically a member of The First Establishment Church but I only go when a friend gets married or an enemy gets buried."

David smiled at the old joke.

"I sorta worship God in my own way," she explained. "What about you?"

"Oh, I've never joined a church."

Joan was happy to hear that.

"Mind you, I'm not against church and I think people should go. Unfortunately in my line of work I'm just too busy."

"What line is that?"

The pilot's voice from the cockpit cut in. "Folks, we're getting ready to make our final approach into Tel Aviv. Please stow your personal belongings and fasten your seat belts. Weather is rainy. We should be on the ground in about thirty minutes."

"So what do you think the odds of a crash landing are now?" David asked.

"Not this again, you're absolutely bonkers," Joan said, rolling her eyes. Nevertheless she took the bait. "Okay, I'd say they're about the same as during take off."

"How about the odds of our jet being hit by a meteor on its final approach?"

"That's actually easier. Some of the big brainiacs figured that out years ago. It's about a billion to one."

"How about the odds of a bird strike disabling one of our engines?"

"Bird strikes? Like those that downed US Airways flight 1549 over the Hudson River?"

He nodded.

"You're hopeless."

But she couldn't resist the challenge.

"Okay," she replied, bouncing the tips of her fingers together. "Depending on migration patterns, the size of the bird, species, wind factors, outside temperature and our altitude, I'd say about ten thousand to one."

"How about a double missile strike taking out both our engines at once?"

She scoffed. "You've just increased the odds to the tenth power, or an octillion to one. That's a one followed by twenty-seven zeros. Do you realize how inconceivable that is?"

"I take that to mean it probably won't happen?"

"The odds are about the same as raising someone from the dead," she chuckled.

"Do you ever think about death?"

Joan shrugged. "Not so much. Maybe if something dramatically raises the odds, like cave diving. But I don't live on the edge. I don't take risks. I'm safety conscious and I never cross the street without looking both ways." She fluttered her eyelashes in mock innocence.

"There's risk in everything we do," David replied. "Abundance Falls is one of the most dangerous cities in the world."

"Sure, but it's an acceptable risk. My sister lives in the tornado capitol of the world. I have a friend who lives in Seattle where volcanoes could erupt at any moment. Heck, we're headed for Israel ground zero for terrorist attacks. What are the odds that we'll be the victim of one?"

"Probably not much."

"Exactly. I have friends in the life insurance business who tell me the actuary tables predict a man should live to be about seventy-six and a woman should live to be about eighty."

David smiled. "I don't need an actuary table to tell me that. The Bible says that the years of a person's life are about seventy and even if they use some unknown power, just eighty."

"I thought you said you don't go to church."

"I don't."

"And you don't follow a religion?"

"Nope, I just think everyone should read the Bible."

"Well all I know is that I'm young and I've got a long life ahead of me."

"That's if you don't experience the God Factor first,"

Sarah interrupted, setting a tray of snacks down on the table between them.

"How do you know about the God Factor?"

Sarah cocked her head. "Didn't you invent the term for your doctoral dissertation? I remember reading your theory that accounted for the whimsical, unpredictable, capricious and random events that seemingly come from out of nowhere to mess up a perfectly good prediction analysis. I believe you were nationally recognized when it was published as, *How the God Factor Impacts Predictive Analysis.*"

Joan stared at Sarah dumbfounded. She couldn't understand how a cabin attendant would know anything about her article.

"But the God Factor is not as whimsical or capricious as you thought," Sarah continued. "Actually nothing in life happens by accident. God doesn't get up in the morning and spin a wheel of chance. Everything is foreknown by God even though humans don't understand how."

Joan thought the conversation had turned creepy.

The plane shuddered and there was an indistinct rumble in the rear cargo area like a large suitcase had toppled over.

The noise startled the three bureaucrats.

"What's going on?" Mr. Black demanded.

"I need a drink," Mr. Brown said, yawning.

"I want an explanation," Ms. Primly commanded.

"All in good time," Sarah answered. "For now, just listen."

The three were not used to being told what to do and

began to object. Sarah lifted a finger and they were instantly silent.

"Explain," Joan asked, her eyes darting around the cabin.

"What you just heard was the sound of the probability of octillion to one," David clarified, calmly.

"What are you talking about?"

"What you heard was the sound of an FIM-91 Stinger missile striking one of our engines."

"A Stinger missile, are you crazy?" Joan's eyes widened in horror. She looked out the window. The rain made visibility difficult.

David calmly reached into his shirt pocket and handed her a plastic credit card. Embossed in gold was the following:

11/30 - 32.070974, 34.741621 - 0930

Joan studied the numbers. "These are times, dates and latitude and longitude coordinates, so what?" She flipped the card down on the table.

"They are the precise date, time and location that the God Factor will change your life." She arched an eyebrow.

David smiled. "You just told us that your actuary tables predict that a female will live to be about eighty years old. However, you of all females failed to account for the God Factor."

"You think you can frighten me with the God Factor? I invented the God Factor, you twit. We're thirty minutes from landing and you're trying to scare me with some sick joke? I'm on my way to an important meeting."

"More important than you know. And in precisely four

minutes fifty-three seconds you will have the most important meeting of your life."

Joan's eyes slid from David to Sarah and then back to David. Their stony expressions didn't flinch or betray their thoughts.

The jet shuddered. A chunk of its disintegrating engine ripped a jagged gash through the rear compartment causing the plane to sharply decelerate and tip downward. The jet was dying. A second blast rattled the plane. Freezing air began swirling around the cabin sucking everything outside not tied down. "Help me!" Ms. Primly screamed, vainly clutching the arm of her chair.

Joan stared at the cockpit hoping the pilots could save the jet. Instead the cockpit door opened and both pilots walked down the aisle toward her.

"Hello mum, remember me?"

Dear God it's Edward the doorman.

"And what about me?" asked Hector the taxi driver, chewing on a toothpick. He reached into the pocket of his shirt. "By the way here's your hundred dollars back."

I'm going insane.

"You were a foolish girl," Sarah scolded mildly. "You loved the world and all the things in it. You worshipped status, statistics, achievements, possessions, ideologies and political causes. If you'd only worshipped Jesus as your God this very day you would inherit a very different life."

"You could have had salvation mum." Edward said, gently.

"You still can," Hector voiced, brightly. "If you just ask for it."

Joan recoiled in disbelief. "Who are you people?"

"WE'RE NOT PEOPLE," Sarah began. She held up a hand and instantly time stopped. Papers flying around the cabin hung motionless in mid air. Coffee spilling sideways across the floor froze in place. Rushing air became still. The jet stopped falling in mid flight.

"We are the four angels of salvation," Sarah said. "We patrol the earth in the name of the Lord reaping his harvest and delivering his souls for judgment. I'm the angel called remorse.

"The Lord sent us in answer to your sister's prayers," David said. "She asked that God would awaken your heart sometime before the end of your life. That sometime is now."

Joan struggled to fight her panic. "My sister prayed for me, why would she do that?"

"Because she loves you."

"Loves me? If she loved me she would do what I say, not plan for my death."

"That's something you should have done."

"Why? I haven't even started to live."

"Oh, but you have lived," David said, pulling a file from his briefcase. "According to my notes you spent your brief life lavishing yourself with expensive trinkets, extravagant self indulgences, trivial awards and an abundance of vanity. All in all, you lived your time on earth wanting for nothing and helping no one but yourself. Do you now regret it?"

Joan didn't understand, what he was asking. "Why would I regret it? I'm popular, successful, educated and rich. What's wrong with that?"

"Nothing," David said. "Every blessing comes from God. It's not his blessings it's what you did with them. For example, why didn't you help Megan and her family with your blessing of great wealth? You certainly complained that they were poor enough."

"Megan would have wasted my money buying junk like this cheesy pot-metal cross." She lifted it from her neck.

"Cheesy?" David asked. "It's because she knew you would never buy one for yourself and she wanted you to have it as a reminder."

"A reminder of what, her red-neck religion?"

"Her love."

"You underestimated Megan," David said. "She's actually exceptionally good with money. She runs her whole family on Doug's modest salary with a little left over for college savings for the kids."

"Look at this," Sarah said, holding up a golden notebook. "It says here that you were embarrassed to tell your friends that you were raised in Nowheresville. You were afraid they would think your family was ignorant and unsophisticated. According to these notes provided by your guardian angel you told people that Doug was in the oil business. When in fact he drives a truck for an oil company."

Joan rejected the claim. "Next you be telling me that you have reports from the tooth fairy, Easter bunny and Santa Claus. Besides, what are you telling me.? Was I was supposed to be proud of growing up in Nowheresville?"

"You might have been proud of your sister."

"Why, Megan could have made something of herself. She threw her life away marrying a man with no ambition, having a couple of rug rats, cleaning house and living in the ass-crack of the country. I tried talking sense to her but she wouldn't listen."

"You're very hard on Megan for a woman who has everything," David said.

"Me have everything, hardly," Joan scoffed.

"I'm speaking about Megan."

Joan jerked back like she'd been slapped in the face. She sat motionless as David continued to speak.

"Megan has all of the things that make a human rich - faith, family and friends. You chose ambition, wealth and recognition. Maybe you should apologize to God for being so stupid."

"To God, for what? Am I supposed to apologize for chasing my dreams and following my heart?"

"No, you're supposed to apologize to God for not chasing his dreams and following his heart."

"God has dreams? Follow God's heart? How's anyone supposed to know what's God's heart or even if he exists? It's not like he makes himself clear."

David leaned closer. "Oh, but he does. Take for instance where your Bible says, 'the heavens declare the glory of God.

Their expanse shows his handiwork. There is no tongue nor language where his voice is not heard.'"

"That's just a figure of speech," Joan replied. "God doesn't talk."

Sarah spoke with compassion, "Of course he talks. It's just that you never learned his language. You studied the language of social acceptance."

"That's crap," Joan objected. "I was a good person. I was a member of First Establishment Church. I gave back to the community."

"There's a big difference between being a good person and being a godly person," David said.

Joan ignored him. "Then why was I honored for my work supporting women's health rights? Forecast Magazine featured my community kindness in a two-page write up. Planned Parenting and the National Abortion Association honored me with awards for supporting women's reproductive rights. I was even on the cover of Fem Magazine because I championed the LGBTQ movement. Don't tell me that I'm not a good person."

Sarah spoke, "Joan, you fancy yourself an enlightened woman. Did you actually believe that a fetus is just an inanimate blob of tissue? Can a man become a woman just by saying so? More than anyone you should know that the scientific probability of that being true is zero."

Sarah made a zero with her fingers.

Joan crossed her arms defiantly. "All enlightened people in Abundance Falls donate to the arts, progressive movements, the support of women's health and LGBTQ rights."

"And they received their praise from men, but not from God."

David spoke, "Yet you deny that you never heard his voice. Were there no stars above your city or did you just never look? And what about your own heart calling you, inviting you, whispering God's love and truth? Your sister tried to awaken you to the illusion of the life you'd created"

"My sister is a religious fanatic," Joan growled, pressing bloodless lips together.

"Your sister," David replied in a measured tone, "isn't perfect, but she loves you. She prays for you every night. Yet you have the arrogance to actually pity her."

"That's not right," Joan stammered, defiantly. "I love my sister, I just can't stand her bigoted religious beliefs. Why would I believe in a good God that lets millions of children starve to death and kills thousands of innocent people in floods and earthquakes? I'd rather believe in the Flying Spaghetti Monster than the writings of a bunch of misogynist old men who wrote the Bible. Jesus' followers have brought more wars and death to the planet than anyone else."

"Actually it's atheism under the guise of communism that has killed the most people," Sarah said. "It's ironic that you spent your short life calculating the probability of every conceivable truth except the truth that God exists."

"The truth that God exists? There's no verifiable truth that God exists."

David responded. "Yes there is," he whispered. "For starters, you could have gone out of your way to do some research, read some books and ask some people. Eventually you would have reached the obvious conclusion that there is a God and you ain't him. At which point you could have reached out."

"How?"

"You could have simply asked God to communicate with you."

"Sure," she said, disdainfully. "Like he's going to take time from his busy schedule to have a little chat with me."

"God always has time for you. If you ask sincerely he will communicate with you in a perceivable way. You can always personally experienced Him for yourself and then you would have tangible proof of his existence - no more speculation, no more guessing."

Sarah injected, "Why not ask him to speak to you right now?"

Joan squirmed. "Why should I? It's a little late for the big man upstairs to start talking to me. Besides, will it keep me from dying right now?"

"No, it will keep you from dying forever."

Joan wasn't used to thinking about God much less striking up a conversation. She had nothing to say.

Sarah raised her hand in peace. "Joan, we're not here to badger you. We're here to help you see the errors you've made in your life. You're a smart woman just don't outsmart yourself. There's no time to save your body but you can still save your soul."

With those words Sarah began shedding her human form to become a breathtaking angelic. Edward and Hector joined her and they all three became magnificent celestial beings.

"Even in your last moments the hand of God is outstretched to receive you contrite heart," David said, his human body melting away. "God's love is greater than all of the waters in the world. Just ask, listen and you can receive his greatest gift."

In spite of the awfulness and the terror in her heart Joan couldn't help thinking that she had never seen anything so dazzling, dreadful or wonderful as these four magnificent angelic messengers who swiftly vanished from her sight.

INSTANTLY, time started again and the jet's fuselage continued to decompose. The engine's turbines tore the cabin apart like a chainsaw ripping through a beer can.

Joan refused to believe what was happening. *Someone drugged me. I'm hallucinating. I'm dreaming. I'll wake up. Four angels of salvation—horse crap!* Her mind scrambled to make logic of the causes and effects that brought this calamity about.

The plane's starboard wing shrieked in a mournful metallic groan as it bent upward and cracked off in one ghastly goodby. The plastic and aluminum fuselage began tumbling across the heavens as Joan watched the earth and sky replace each other again and again while strapped to her seat.

Yet she still rejected the truth.

She cursed.

This is crap. No one deserves this. What kind of God sends angels to help a person then lets them die? If God can talk why doesn't he come down from heaven and do it?

After a few seconds she realized she was just howling at the moon. And for a moment she experienced a sense of peace.

Okay, okay, maybe I was a little hasty. Maybe God exists. Angels are real. I saw them didn't I? They tried to help me. Maybe I've been wrong.

She realized she was freezing. She hugged herself tightly. She wished she'd kept her jacket on. Where the hell was her hat? *What if I apologize to God? What are the odds he'd get me out of this?*

She began weeping.

I'll be nicer to Megan. I'll start going to church. I'll give away my car. I'll move out of the condo. I'll donate to religious charities. I'll pay to send Megan's kids to college. I mean it. I'm sorry - sorry - sorry.

The aircraft suddenly disintegrated into a thousand pieces and Joan was ejected into the icy atmosphere still strapped firmly in her seat. Her mind was a bubbling caldron of thoughts - frothing, and churning like the whitecaps in the sea below. Her face was a hideous mask of fear. Her mind kept trying to make logic of the probabilities that had brought about this calamity. She kept repeating a mantra of words she'd been taught by her spiritual masters. *What have I done, I have done nothing, I am the victim of coincidence, what have I done, I have done nothing, I am the victim of coincidence.*

She surveyed the glimmering cobalt blue water stretching a thousand feet beneath her feet. The sun was beginning to set in the west. For the first time in her life she saw past the equations, philosophies, causes and trinkets that had filled her world. Suddenly she had a clear understanding that beyond all of her human imagination it was too late. She'd pursued the things of the world and now the world was gone.

The rushing wind caused her seat to abruptly tilt backward forcing her to look upwards at the mantle of tiny stars twinkling against dark deep space above her. It was true, God's voice had always been pouring forth out of the heavens. Even now he was within reach but Joan was too panicked to think of prayer. The ocean below was a caldron of tiny whitecaps frothing and dotting the churning sea. Joan was totally and horribly alone.

Like a human meteor she shot out of the heavens towards the ocean amid a sky filled with airplane junk. She had nothing to say, not a word and not a prayer formed upon her lips. It briefly crossed her mind asking what the odds were of surviving this mess. But she realized the odds were zero, naught, nil. As she neared terminal velocity of about three hundred miles per hour she saw a small fleet of fishing boats on the choppy surface.

She wondered how long she would have to swim before being rescued. She wondered if it was better to keep her boots on or get rid of them. She tried to remember where Sarah said they kept the lifejackets. She imagined news crews waiting to interview her. Then it suddenly occurred to her that Megan wasn't the one who was insane, she was.

What kind of a lunatic keeps analyzing the odds of surviving this? What's wrong with me? How can I believe this will turn out all right? I'm pathetic. Sweet Jesus - Jesus - Jesus, I'm screwed. I've been living in the land of Pretendia.

She began laughing in crazy spasms.

The phone in her hand vibrated. She didn't care.

On the Eastern horizon the Tel Aviv skyline rose up like fingers in prayer. A single beam of sunshine reached out and momentarily touched her face. Then she heard the far away voice of her mother singing an old church hymn.

"*Amazing grace, how sweet the sound . . .*

Like a lonely meteor Joan shot from the heavens towards the earth. Above her face a mantle of tiny stars twinkled against the cobalt blue of deep space.

. . . That saved a wretch like me . . .

She realized it was true. God's voice did pour out of the heavens. He had always been communicating with her. For the first time in her life she saw past the equations, philosophies, and social causes that filled her world.

. . . I once was lost but now I'm found . . .

At a thousand feet over the bay she reached terminal velocity of three hundred miles per hour. Her freezing lips tried to form a prayer.

... was blind, but now I see ...

At five hundred feet she saw an orange rescue boat jetting across the water towards her anticipated crash site. It's trailing wake of white foam looked like an arrow pointing to her doom.

... 'Twas grace that taught my heart to fear ...

At four hundred feet she saw a man standing on the deck of a fishing boat aiming his smartphone at her. His video would go viral tonight.

... and grace my fears relieved ...

At three hundred feet she accepted her imminent death. She watched numbly as the water quickly approached.

... How precious did that grace appear ...

At two hundred feet Joan began weeping hysterically.

... the hour I first believed ...

At one hundred feet she began screaming for God.

Two days later scuba divers of the Israeli Navy found the plane's wreckage. Master Diver Jacob Cohen surfaced to report that the mortal remains of Joan Dodson were quietly resting in about a hundred feet of murky water. She was still tightly buckled into her plush leather seat. Both arms had come to rest in her lap, her golden hair waved languidly with the currents, her chin tilted down upon her chest and her eyes closed as if she was in prayer. In one of her hands she gripped a cell phone and in the other she clutched a small silver cross. He also reported that despite his best efforts he couldn't find a trace of the other passengers or crew.

What he did find that he did not report was an image that would haunt him for the rest of his life. For there in the gloomy depths of the water where shadows play tricks on a diver's mind and the currents create ghostly illusions, he swore it looked like she was smiling.

2
THE INVISIBLE WOMAN

Everyone knew there was something wrong with Sergeant McKenna. It was no secret that she struggled with inner ghosts and fears, but who doesn't? So we didn't take her problems too seriously. Looking back I wish we did. I'm haunted by the lingering sadness in her eyes and the faint melancholy that shrouded her smile. Signs that should have told me that her problems were deeper.

IF YOU'RE ASKING who I am there's not much to say. I grew up in the sprawling mess of the West Valley of Los Angeles. My dad travelled for a living so I didn't see much of him as a kid. My mom stayed at home raising my sister and me. When I was a senior in high school my dad took me aside put an arm around my shoulder and told me that I had three options when I graduated. One, go to college which we knew we couldn't afford. Two, enlist in the military and get paid for Uncle Sam would pay for my college. Three get a job and pay for my own bills.

I'm a reasonably smart guy so I chose option number two. I drove to the local recruiting station tucked away in a squalid strip mall in my neighborhood. All five of the military services were crammed into a space roughly the size of five metal desks, a water cooler and a bathroom. When I walked through the door they all looked up in mild astonishment. Southern California wasn't exactly the enlistment capitol of the world. One had his boots on his desk, another looked like he was playing Tetris on his phone, one was pouring himself a cup of coffee and another other was exiting the latrine.

I stepped around the Marine, Coast Guard and Navy out of courtesy to my stomach. Large posters of floating Aircraft Carriers and Marine amphibious tanks were enough to make me queasy. The Air Force guy didn't even bother to say hello. I found out later that he had a long waiting list of guys who'd heard life in the Air Force was easy. That left the Army who shouted from the coffee machine for me to sit down. Which I did. I've always been good at taking orders. Balancing a frosted donut on the top of his coffee mug emblazoned with "This We'll Defend" he stepped to his desk. "You looking for the danger of an Airborne Ranger?" He didn't bat an eye.

"No I want to serve but I don't want to get my ass shot off."

"Who does?" he said, smiling. "Unfortunately not many

jobs like that in the Army." Then out of the blue he asked me, "Did you know that the Army has more boats than the Navy? How about something to do with boats?"

"Did you not just see me walk past the Navy and Coast Guard?"

He took a sip of his coffee and looked at me seriously. "You religious?" he asked, gravely.

"Not especially," I answered.

"Good, I got the perfect job for you. Let's make you a Chaplain Assistant."

He could see by the look on my face that I'd never heard of such a thing.

"A chaplain is like a minister down at the local church only he's in the Army. You'll be assigned to set up for his worship services, counseling sessions, manage his office, print bulletins and drive his vehicle — that sort of thing."

"Like a special assistant?"

"And because the chaplain doesn't carry a weapon in combat, you'll be trained to be his body guard."

I frowned.

"Don't worry you'll spend most of your enlistment in the air-conditioned comfort of a cozy chapel. Whaddya say?"

"No danger?"

"Only if you get deployed and the chaplain decides to go outside the wire which they rarely do."

"Can I jump out of an airplane?

"Absolutely we'll send you to Airborne school."

"Sign me up," I said immediately.

It wasn't long before I was at Fort Jackson roaming the hallowed halls of the Chaplain School. Brother did I wake up in a hurry. When I wasn't in a class listening to an instructor droning on about how to light a candle stick I was listening to a Baptist chaplain bicker about Presbyterians complaining about the Episcopalians who looked down their nose at the Lutherans who ignored the Adventists who avoided the Fundamentalists who hated the Catholics who snubbed everyone.

I was beginning to wonder what I'd gotten myself into.

Soon enough I was assigned to the 28th Military Police Battalion in the 74th MP Brigade where I met the freshly minted First Lieutenant Chaplain Curtis Haws. Haws had found his divine calling as an Army Chaplain after failing as the pastor of several small rural churches. At the age of thirty-six the faithful fundamentalist had seen the light and found Uncle Sam as his worldly savior. Now he could concentrate on getting the Army saved.

I caught him as he was leaving the PX.

"Morning sir," I said, snapping a crisp salute. For a moment he looked like he didn't know what to do. Then he hesitantly raised his left arm and returned it to his side. I didn't correct him figuring it might be too early in our budding relationship to explain that he'd saluted with his wrong hand.

"Morning," he said, as if he was trying to place my face.

"I'm your new chaplain assistant," I said, trying to help him. "Private First Class Chad Adams.

"Of course," he mumbled. "Just call me Pastor Curtis."

"Sir? You're an officer."

"I don't like the military formality," he said, hefting a large Bible he carried under his arm. "I want soldiers to think of me as their friend not as their officer. I've been sent here to save souls for Jesus not to command them. I think it's best if I'm considered one of the troops if you know what I mean."

I didn't know what he meant or even if he did officers were never expected to be on informal terms with the troops. This was a different take on what I'd been taught as an enlisted man.

"You a Christian?" he asked, looking me up and down like a cook appraising the catch of the day. "Have you been saved by the blood of Jesus Christ and accepted him as your Lord and Savior?"

I suddenly regretted enlisting as a chaplain assistant.

"Well, never mind," he said, abruptly. "We'll have plenty of time to talk when we get to Iraq. By the way we're deploying next month."

You cannot imagine my joy at the thought of a year in combat with Chaplain Haws.

And deploy we did. We packed a shit-ton of King James Bibles because Chaplain Haws said it was the only true Bible.

We boxed thousands of Chick tracts, religious brochures, salvation pamphlets written in English and Arabic and booklets of faith from his denomination. Thankfully his worship beliefs didn't include candles, wine, communion wafers, statues, vestments and music. I asked what he planned to do with all of his religious stuff and he said, "Everyone needs to read the holy word of truth found in the Bible." By everyone I assumed he meant the six million people living around Baghdad.

WE ARRIVED in mid June and settled into a daily routine of doing pretty much the same thing, nothing. After a couple of weeks, one of our guys got killed. The story was that Specialist Tony Jankowski was in the turret of his Humvee leaning over the edge throwing candy to kids running along side when he'd been shot through the neck by a sniper. That's when we learned that our enemy had no problem using children as bait. None of the officers had to say it — we stopped throwing candy.

The rear eschaton fobbits sitting at Division HQ in air-conditioned comfort loudly complained saying we needed to show our friendliness to the locals. Seemed our decision to survive by not throwing candy to the kids didn't fit in with their latest psyop slogan "Together We are Stronger." Combat veterans know that war is ninety-nine percent bullshit coming from the higher command and one percent bullshit coming from the enemy.

The good chaplain was told to conduct Jankowski's

memorial ceremony. The learned man of God objected saying that his fundamentalist beliefs wouldn't allow him to conduct a ceremony unless Jankowski was a born again, river baptized Christian. And not just any born again river baptized Christian, but an Independent Fundamentalist Evangelical Missionary Christian.

The Battalion Commander shot off like a bottle rocket and after a couple of painful ass chewing's a few phone calls to the Brigade Chaplain's office, several heated discussions with Haws denominational representative and a dozen exchanges with the Chief of Chaplain's office it was decided that the Brigade Chaplain would conduct the ceremony. If Chaplain Curtis wanted everyone to call him by his first name he'd certainly gotten his wish, except Curtis wasn't the name they were calling him.

After that our Battalion Commander had nothing to do with Chaplain Haws. It was just as well. Lieutenant Colonel Philip "Skip" Prescott was the kind of guy who loved to beat up on people. He got a perverse pleasure humiliating his captains during their daily updates, especially the females who he regularly invited to his office for "senior mentoring." We all knew it was just an opportunity for him to see who would bend over and take his abuse.

DURING ONE OF our evening staff updates Prescott interrogated Chaplain Haws about religious support issues. He asked technical questions no first term chaplain would know. After about three minutes of examination Haws was so confused and embarrassed that he fell into numbed silence. It was painful to watch. The rest of the staff stared at their boots knowing their turn might be next. If Prescott had no mercy for a man of God we were all screwed.

Prescott had no respect for chaplains and Haws had validated his feelings. I remember when Haws first reported for duty Prescott told him in front of the staff, "If you don't have anything to do, don't do it here." Haws took it as an order and disappeared.

Eventually our battle rhythm picked up and the meetings intensified. Haws attendance at the gatherings grew less and less until eventually his absence wasn't even noticed. As long as he stayed out of trouble Prescott didn't care what Haws did or where he did it.

Haws took his banishment well. He seemed to have no idea his military career hung in the balance. All he fixated on was the fact that he was headed for glory with or without me or you. I once found him reciting Bible verses over and over like a child on the spectrum. Worse, he seemed strangely happy that he was mocked, scorned and ridiculed. "They treated Jesus like this," he confided, proudly. Such was the canting cultic cocoon he lived in.

ONE DAY, bored out of my mind I was sweeping the Mesopotamian dust off the floor of the chapel when in walks the Battalion Sergeant Major Lance Spears. He never came to the chapel — ever. I was suddenly concerned that my mom had died.

"Where's your chaplain?"

I stood erect holding my broom at parade rest.

"Out doing ministry of presence Sergeant Major."

"Ministry of presence," he scoffed, what the shit is that?"

"It means that God goes where ever he goes."

"You saying that whenever the chaplain walks around that God magically does some sort of ministry?"

"Sort of."

"Who makes this crap up?"

"Chaplain School."

"Your chaplain is like God alright," he said. "He's often talked about, never seen and nobody knows what the fuck he does."

That's why Lance Spears was a Battalion Sergeant Major.

He glanced around the empty chapel. "I don't think Chaplain Haws knows what to do with you, but I do. I need a shooter down at the 872nd MP company and you're qualified. Grab your stuff and report to Sergeant First Class McConnell. You'll be assigned to Sergeant Taylor's squad. Any questions?"

"What about Chaplain Haws?" I asked, looking around at my comfortable and safe workplace. For the first time in my life I said a little prayer. Maybe Haw's religion was rubbing off on me.

"The good padre has no objections," Spears said, smiling widely. "He was more than happy to throw you under the bus. Just pack your shit and be ready to move out tomorrow morning."

I was slightly hurt that Chaplain Haws hadn't put up a fight to keep me. But then the poor chaplain barely knew what to do with himself much less me. My reassignment meant one less problem for him.

That's how I ended up sitting in the turret of an up-armored humvee at Bagdad International Airport on a smoking hot day with my glove resting on the receiver of a Browning .50 cal. machine gun waiting for Sergeant Sally McKenna to arrive.

"Adams," Sergeant Taylor yelled from the command seat. "Want some Gatorade?"

"I'm good," I replied. "Any ice water?"

He rummaged around in the truck's ice chest before shouting, "Negatory, all gone." After a thousand bottles of Florida's favorite drink it turned out that good old ice water was still the best refreshment.

I sighed, it would be nice if the daily shuttle from Kuwait came early. Every day a lumbering C-130 brought an assortment of contractors, reporters, troops and other personnel who needed to get to the war zone. Then it would turn right around and take another assortment of straphangers back to Kuwait where they would hop on an Air Force plane headed to the U.S., Germany or elsewhere. Unfortunately I wasn't going with them.

Minutes ticked off in the 120* degree heat. Perspiration ran down my back until it found my crack and flowed down to tickle the family jewels. I tried to think of anything else but the torment.

Eventually I spotted a tiny black dot falling out of the southeastern sky. I squinted and watched it begin executing a series of evasive maneuvers meant to avoid enemy insurgents on the ground. Up, down, right, left, it was like watching a rollercoaster threading its way through a mine field. I knew it was horrible for those on board. Months ago I'd taken the same ride. Rumor had it that sometimes the Air Force pilots liked to throw in a few extra ups and downs just to be ornery.

It landed and the sound of its reverse thrusters signaled it had touched down safely. In the distance the pilot taxied towards us. When he got close enough he swung the plane around kicking up a blinding dust storm. He lowered the tail ramp without bothering to shut down the engines. He throttled back just enough to let his human cargo disembarked on wobbly legs. He had no intention of waiting very long. Air Force pilots didn't like to spend a minute away from their comforts in Kuwait. And sure as heck Bagdad International didn't have any of the comforts they were used to.

Two columns of personnel began filing down the ramp in neat and orderly fashion. Even from a distance I could tell a soldier from a contractor. Something in the way a soldier carried themselves. But mostly in the fact that soldiers don't usually have beer bellies. From where we sat everyone was just a moving silhouette. Lucky for us at six foot-four

Sergeant Sally McKenna stood head and shoulders above everyone. It was like spotting a bumblebee in an ant colony.

From time to time she'd look around cautiously as if she might have to whip out a salute for some eager officer. But after one look at Sergeant McKenna you knew that only a butter bar Lieutenant with a death wish would be dumb enough try and pull rank. Not that there weren't plenty of dumb lieutenants – Derrick Ortiz, our platoon leader being one of them.

None of us got out of the vehicle. I waved to get her attention and thumbed with a gloved hand to the seat beneath me. Being our vehicle was the only one painted with Military Police on the side she threw her duffle bag over one shoulder, grabbed another with a meaty fist and lugged them over.

"Welcome to Iraq," I shouted over the roar of the C-130's turbo props. McKenna nodded and tossed her crap into the rear compartment. Then she expertly folded her gigantic body into the cramped back seat, her knees practically touching her chin. Our driver, Pfc. Lopez then wheeled us out of there like we'd been summoned to a bank robbery.

SHE WAS strange and oddly inspiring. She looked like Le Braun James in drag. Her hands were the size of oven mittens, her arms reached her knees, a brushy unibrow dragged across her forehead like one long caterpillar, her black hair was cornrowed and her lower lip protruded so far out it gave the impression that she was chewing on an inner tube when she spoke. She was no looker.

It's not like the Army doesn't have its share of uglies, weirdo's, eccentrics and sociopaths, yours truly being one. So, I liked her from the moment she reached up into the turret and swallowed my hand shaking it. Yep, Sgt. McKenna was in a league of her own.

Under normal conditions a person her of her size might have been rejected by the recruiters, but these weren't normal times. We'd been at war for several years and it didn't look like it would let up any time soon. I figured some recruiter down in Baton Rouge thought he'd pulled three 7s when Sally walked in. She was female, she was a minority and most important she was willing to fight Uncle Sam's enemies.

Born on the banks of the Louisiana swamps Sally was raised a proper Christian girl by a decorated Viet Nam vet and his church going wife. She watched her father fight his last battle with the Veterans Administration trying to obtain treatment for the cancer he'd received from exposure to Agent Orange in Viet Nam. But the VA kept denying his claim until he finally died at the age of fifty-eight leaving her mom a grieving widow struggling to raise three children. Had it not been for the members of her church, the Ebenezer African Congregational Tabernacle they might not have made it. Sally was in high school and completely heartbroken.

But she was a fighter and went on to play state level basketball during her sophomore year driving for fifty-eight points against Shreveport in the state finals. At her father's passing she'd already been named athlete of the year twice by Sports Play Magazine. The offers began pouring in from the top women's basketball teams at LSU and Baylor, but she declined.

You might be asking yourself why a superstar like Sally rejected scholarships to schools like Baylor and LSU. I mean, what kind of crazy person would turn down an offer to play for a top NCAA team? Well, it turns out that Sally was a woman of character and a patriot right down to the Cajun marrow in her Tabasco filled bones. When America was attacked on 9-11 Sally said she knew what to do — she had to defend her country.

With her mom's blessing and a kiss, Sally enlisted right out of high school and was sent to basic training. That's where the U.S. Army discovered that Sally wasn't exactly their normal kind of recruit. She could bench press her own weight, run two miles without breaking a sweat, field strip an M4 carbine with both eyes shut and shoot expert with her pistol. The doctors gave her a body fat test and discovered that she was almost pure muscle.

From there she was off to Military Police training at Fort Leonard Wood where she smoked her classes. Unsurprisingly she was named the distinguished graduate. I decided to stay on the good side of Sgt. McKenna.

We convoyed back to the company area on Camp Liberty and dropped her among the waiting female members of the unit. We left her standing like an ebony Gulliver surrounded by a dozen Lilliputians wearing camouflage uniforms.

FOR THE ONE

A MILITARY POLICE unit isn't exactly what you'd call the pointy tip of the spear, meaning that we don't have to ruck-march for hours or breach doorways. Our life is a lot more comfortable than the average grunt. We ride wherever we go, live in air-conditioned prefab trailers, eat at the big mess hall and surf the net at the free Internet café. Life was pretty good except for our trips outside the wire.

Things went back to normal and we checked off a couple of months on the calendar. I'd see Chaplain Haws from time to time in the dining facility trying to evangelize the heathen troops with his "do you know where your soul is going if you got killed tonight?" He was as welcomed as head lice.

The dining facility was about the size of an airplane hanger. A thousand guys could select from a cornucopia of culinary delights. It was a glutton's heaven. Roast beef, chicken, ham, BBQ ribs and chops, salads of every kind, mixed green, three bean and carrot, potatoes whipped, fried, baked and mashed. And deserts - seriously? Pies, cakes, frozen treats, cabinets of ice cream and trays of yogurt. And plenty of protein bars and cereal boxes to stuff in our cargo pockets to take with us. I began to worry that the biggest threat to my life was dying of a heart attack or diabetes. Most guys gained about twenty pounds before their tour was over.

We grabbed a table and cradled our bounty before us. Nobody said grace and we started eating.

"So what you make about Sergeant McKenna?" Sergeant Taylor asked.

"Big," I mumbled, through a mouth full of spaghetti.

"Big is an understatement," Pfc. Lopez nodded, pushing food around his plate.

"Let's call her Big Sally," I offered.

Taylor chewed thoughtfully. "Yeah, Big Sally, sounds good."

"Maybe she'd be offended," Private Wilson offered. "How about polk Sally, like the song?"

"The song was called Polk Salad not Polk Sally you moron."

Wilson shrugged. "Still?"

"What if she complains we're making fun of her?" Lopez asked, always the voice of reason.

"Then she don't get a nickname," Sgt. Taylor said, placing his utensils down, indicating that the polls were closed on the subject. Big Sally it was. Better than nothing. Having no nickname was the ultimate social snub.

ANOTHER MONTH ROLLED by and we heard rumors that Big Sally was being assigned from Battalion HQ to our team. It looked like Sargent Major Spears was finally going to replace me with a fully qualified MP. I couldn't hide my glee.

"I bet you're thinking that your gonna to go back to that nice air conditioned chapel of yours?" Spears asked. "I mean we wouldn't want the good chaplain to loose track of any of his pew Bibles would we?"

I nodded weakly knowing what was coming.

"Not going to happen," he said, matter of factly. "You're staying right here."

"But Sergeant Major, I'm a chaplain assistant not a qualified MP."

"You're what the Army says you are. And the Army says it needs you more as a bullet shooter than Chaplain Haws does. Besides, you're actually a pretty good soldier, you fit in with the team and the guys trust your judgment."

I thought about his flattery for a moment.

"And most importantly you're qualified to drive."

He scratched his chin. "I'll tell you what. I'll have you rotate with Pfc. Lopez and we'll put McKenna up in the turret."

I knew it was the best deal I would get. I took it without objection. Chaplain Haws would just have to get along without me, not that he cared.

It was Sunday morning when Big Sally reported to our team. We were getting ready to head outside the wire to check on some Iraqi police stations. The Brigade had been training them for months and we made regular rounds to evaluate their progress. Our first stop was at one of their stations in Sadr City, a suburb of Bagdad. We all knew the ride might get a little dicey. Sadr City had been the center of some fierce fighting and dying. We were all hyped. We'd be moving in a three-vehicle convoy with us in the middle. We assembled in front of the battalion motor pool which was directly across from the chapel. I eyed my former workplace like an alcoholic in need of a drink.

Haw's nine o'clock service was just ending and his entire congregation of four soldiers came stumbling outside shielding their eyes from the glare of the sun. Temperatures were already moving into triple digits.

Chaplain Haws caught a glimpse of us going through our pre-convoy checklist and saw an opportunity to do some impromptu preaching to a captive audience. "PFC Adams, long time no see," he said, walking up to my vehicle. "Wish you were back at my side like Saint Paul and Timothy." He grinned his best church smile and looked around at the troops preparing to mount up. Thankfully nobody took his hootenanny holiness seriously.

"You folks going on patrol?" he asked. I wanted to say we were going to a Texas Bar-B-Que but I dummied up. No one ever knew how to respond to his stupid questions. There was an awkward silence until Sgt. Taylor spoke up. "Roger that, sir," he said. Taylor would make a fine diplomat.

"None of us knows the appointed hour of our death," Haws began, soberly. "Is there's any of you who would like to confide a special message to pass on to your loved one in the event you don't return today?" Chaplain sunshine looked around expectantly. "It's alright for you to be afraid. We can walk over to the chapel and you can tell me privately."

No one volunteered.

He reached into his cargo pocket and produced some colorful tracks on death, dying and the afterlife. "Take one of these," he said, passing them out. Nobody wanted one but there's not much an enlisted man can do when an officer shoves something in your face.

Then, in a deep suffering voice of one crying in the wilderness Big Sally stood up in our vehicle's turret raised her arm and bellowed like a tent revivalist. "We ain't afraid of no devil, preacher. Praise da Lord, amen Jesus and amen! We all protected by the blood of Christ. Every soldier here is anointed by his grace and he hath sent forth his mighty angels to make straight our pathway. Praise da Lord!"

Sunglasses were pulled down, mouths gaped open and every soldier turned and looked at her like she was possessed. Except for the day when we'd said hello at the airport I'd never heard the woman speak more than two words. She was awesome – a modern day Joan of Arc protecting us from the chaplain. Haws was visibly stunned and then he shouted to her like they'd been separated at birth. "Amen sister, McKenna. Oh sweet Jesus, thank you for sending us this precious child of God to the land of the Bible. Amen and hallelujah!"

Before he could say another word Big Sally said, "Now let us bow our heads and pray." Which we all did. And in less than thirty seconds Big Sally invoked every blessing of protection for us, our families, our nation, Iraq, the President, congress, the lost, the damned, the found and an assortment of others. It was a beautiful thing. I glanced over at Sgt. Taylor who gave me a sly thumbs up. Big Sally had saved the day. She had skillfully cut-off whatever salvation sermon the chaplain had planned to deliver.

"It grieves me I can't ride along with you fine troops," he

said. "But you know the commandment of God says I must keep Sunday holy and meditate on the Scriptures." I threw up a little in my mouth. Everyday was Sunday according to the chaplains.

"Roger that sir," nodded Sgt. Taylor in a tone that had suddenly become pious. Taylor hadn't earned his stripes for nothing

Just then, 2Lt. Derrick Ortiz stepped out of the lead vehicle and walked back to ours with a scowl on his face. He saluted the chaplain and then promptly ignored him. He turned to Sgt. Taylor. "Can I talk to you for a moment?" It wasn't a question. The rest of us went back to what we were doing and the chaplain left. "What the hell is wrong with Sergeant McKenna is she some sort of religious nut?"

"I don't think so," Taylor said. "I think she just saved us all from the good chaplain."

"Keep an eye on her," Ortiz instructed. "I don't want any swamp loons in my platoon, is that clear?"

"Roger that, sir." Taylor said, saluting and Ortiz stomped back to his vehicle before yelling. "Mount up!"

We donned our Kevlar helmets and I jumped behind the wheel. Taylor sat next to me, Lopez behind me and Big Sally perched her ample rump on the turret's sling-seat.

I IGNITED the hummer's glow plugs, waited for the light to go out, twisted the start lever and cranked it up. The deep throaty rumble of its 6.5-liter turbocharged diesel made a

growling sound reminiscent of a lion stalking its prey. We rolled out of the motor pool kicking up thick clouds of dust. I thought about Chaplain Haws. We didn't need him to remind us of the dangers we faced. The finger of death in Iraq was anywhere and everywhere. I'd been here when twenty guys were blown up eating in the chow hall. I'd heard of one guy watching a USO show taking a bullet in his chest from a firefight going on a half mile outside the perimeter. It made no sense. It wasn't like in the movies where the hero faces the enemy sitting on top of a hill or across a river. In Iraq there was no front line. Draw a three-foot circle around yourself and everything outside was the frontline. In Iraq the moment you left the camp, every car, truck, donkey cart, kid, old man or woman might kill you. Or they could be a spotter, a sniper, a suicide bomber. Then again maybe they were just an innocent civilian. You never knew and there was no way to tell them apart. Women wearing burkas were the most dangerous. They could conceal a suicide vest and you'd never know it until they blew up your world.

For me, the toughest part was the tension caused by the suspense of waiting. You never knew if today was your day. A guy could get killed on his first patrol, his last patrol or anywhere in between. There was nothing you could do to improve or diminish your odds. We used to say it wasn't *if*, but *when* and how bad.

Every death had some some heart-breaking back-story. Pfc. Thomas was killed the day his wife gave birth to his son, Spc. Paulson got sick so Pfc. Martin got killed because she volunteered to take his place on a patrol. Spc. Halston was hitching a ride to some location when his hummer was hit an IED. Sgt. Solomon was celebrating his wedding anniversary and Pfc. Dixon was going on leave the next day. It was misery upon misery. I once heard of a guy who went out side the wire over three hundred times during two deployments and never had a shot fired at him anger. Go figure. It was hard not to become a fatalist.

Maybe if Chaplain Haws had ridden with us a few times he would have learned that real prayer took place in the silence between the moments we rolled out of the company area until we returned to the gates of the camp. Once we left the safety of the camp it was game time — we were too busy trying to stay alive to pray. It was time for the enemy to pray.

Sgt. Taylor keyed his mike, "McKenna you are freaking awesome!"

There was silence for a beat until she replied in her country accent. "Well, sergeant, I's raised in south LA so I's known a lot of little skinny preachers like Haws. Is about scalps. All he wants is for you say what he wants you to say. So I done said it. Save us all a bunch of trouble. If I hadn't said it he'd have kept us there all morning."

I pressed the mike. "So it was all just an act?"

"Mostly," she replied. "I do believe in prayer. But I jazzed it up sows he'd think we'd all just finished a revival meeting."

"McKenna you're amazing."

Lopez jumped in. "Did you say that you were raised in South LA? I got an uncle works in downtown Los Angeles."

"I didn't say that," chuckled Big Sally. "I said South LA. That's LA as in Loo-ee-zee-ana."

We all laughed. The girl had a sense of humor, always a good sign.

"So how's 'bout you guys," she asked. "Tell me 'bout yourselves."

"Not much to say," Sergeant Taylor said. "I'm a career guy. I got a wife and two kids. Born and raised in Birmingham, Alabama and I bleed crimson and white — Roll Tide!"

"Roll Tide!" everyone shouted back.

"I'm from Brooklyn," Lopez said. "I'm single, I'm our resident Mexican, I love the Yankees and I was at NYU studying applied psychology when Haji hit the Towers."

"NYU?" Sally said, in amazement. "I thought they was a bunch of left wing commies. How'd you end up in the Army?"

"Simple," Lopez replied. "My uncle Alberto was in the North Tower when the first plane struck."

There was a respectful silence. "Bible says an eye for an eye, blood for blood. I am here for my uncle Alberto and the others."

It wasn't the first time I'd heard Lopez tell the story but each time I felt a chill go up my arm. When he finished I told Big Sally about myself. When I was done she and Taylor entertained us with stories about the WNBA and college basketball.

Most people think that military police run around the battlefield handing out parking tickets, like civilian cops. Not exactly. My squad was responsible for conducting area security which meant a lot more than sitting around eating donuts. It isn't easy keeping the peace when all the locals are trying to kill you. On top of that, after Saddam was overthrown the Washington whiz-kids failed to take into account that without a working government to maintain control, all the criminals, perverts, mental patients and other assorted crooks and zanies were released onto the streets. Organized crime took over at every level, black market activities created dangerous shadowy subcultures, armed insurgents from Iran and other countries flooded in to take advantage of the situation. Additionally we were tasked to corral the local political and tribal groups who fought everyone for control over the city.

On second thought it sounds exactly like what the Chicago police face every day. Nevertheless it was like trying to referee a cage match where all the players had guns and bombs. We wanted to help the people of Iraq but we didn't want to get killed doing it.

Couple of days later I ran into Colonel Prescott's driver Specialist Alvin Lee. He looked like a refrigerator with arms. "Al, what's going on with pretty boy?" We called Prescott pretty boy because of his whitened teeth and a head of hair he meticulously brushed and gelled. At forty-eight Prescott remained a chiseled physical specimen thanks to a religious regimen of two hours in the gym and two miles of jogging around the camp every morning. Back in the day he played on the Army football team where he made a few memorable plays.

"Prescott's a fast tracker," Al said. "I've watched him suck the lips off the Brigade Commander's eagle." Then he added with a lisp, "Besides, he's got those rugged metrosexual looks and marketable hints of some indefinable ethnic culture that gives him the appearance of a eugenically bred poster boy for the United Nations."

We laughed, we both knew Prescott would go far.

"Is he still preaching the holy gospel of football?"

"Like he was Vince Lombardy himself," Al said. "I'm lucky I played tackle in Junior College so I can talk sports with him. The other morning just for fun I brought up the recent NFL sex scandal and he damn near blew a gasket. 'Throw every one of them perverts in jail. Anyone who betrays the team needs to be punished.'"

"The guy's intense," I said.

"You don't know the half of it. His whole thing is about the team, being on the team, honoring the team, never disgracing the team. What he really means is his team."

THE NEXT DAY we rolled out again. This time we were headed for the Baghdad police academy to assist in training Iraqi police recruits. It was a relatively short run but we took it seriously. The Iraqi police had been the favorite target of insurgent attacks and they'd lost over a thousand officers from snipers and bombings.

"Okay everybody, let's look alive," Taylor said, firmly over the intercom. "The Iraqi police just took a hit from a car bomber last night and word has it they expect more. Big Sally, keep your eyes open for any vehicles that look suspicious. Adams, stay on the lead vehicle and be prepared for evasive maneuvers. Lopez get ready to dismount on my command." We were always glad for another simple assignment.

PART II

My name is Specialist Thad Parker. I work in the office of the Battalion Commander. My background is not important. What is important is that about halfway through our tour I got a call early one Sunday morning.

"Office of the Battalion Commander, Specialist Parker, may I help you sir or ma'am?"

"Hey bro, tell pretty-boy we just had a suicide."

I knew it was Lopez the instant I heard his accent.

"Holy shit! Who was it?"

"Don't know man. Might'a been Sergeant McKenna. They can't make a positive ID 'cause most of the face is missing."

"Jeez — are you sure it's McKenna?"

"Pretty sure, man. All they're sayin' is that it's a black female. Captain Anderson is with the body right now waiting for the CID to show up."

"Thanks buddy, I'll let the boss know."

I double-timed down to Prescott's hooch where I knew he'd be watching Sunday football. Even though he pretended to be a big Christian I'd never seen him at any of the chaplain's services. Banging on his trailer door I stuck my head in.

Pretty boy was pacing around the room yelling at a cell phone. A football game was blaring on the TV in the background. "Look son, you need come to Iraq and get into the game," he said. "You don't want the brass to think you're a friggen loser do you?"

Prescott's shy son was nothing like his driven father who'd badgered him into playing competitive sports, finagled him a slot at West Point and expected him to take a commission in the Infantry when he graduated - which he did - reluctantly. Now, Captain Philip Prescott Jr. was serving safely at a desk job at Picatinny Arsenal, hardly a career enhancing position.

"I'll pull some strings and get you a nice meaty assignment,"Prescott said. He listened for a moment then barked, "I don't want to hear another damn word out of your mouth. You're coming to Iraq and that's it." He pocketed the cell phone, checked the score of the game and turned to me. "What's up peewee?" I hated him calling me peewee but I kept my mouth shut. "Bad news sir, we had a suicide this morning. Don't know who it was 'cause they say most of the face is gone. They think it might be Sergeant McKenna."

"Who?"

"You remember, sir. She used to be down in Headquarters Company."

"Oh yeah the baboon from the lagoon. Has anyone else been informed?" A trace of fear flashed across his gunmetal eyes. We both knew the Army liked to blame commanders for suicides. "Not from me, sir."

"Excellent, get with Captain Anderson and find out the last time he did a suicide brief for the soldiers. And find Chaplain Haws - tell him to get down there and do some of his magic."

Nice touch I thought. Sending for the chaplain would

give the right appearance and check all the blocks. Only one problem.

"Sir, the chaplain is setting up for his religious service right now."

"I don't care if he's counseling Jesus Christ. You tell him to get his fat ass down there."

I left Prescott yelling at something on the television and I headed down to the chapel.

I FOUND Chaplain Haws placing a Bible on each chair of those he prayed would show up to his worship service. "The Colonel wants you to get down to the 872nd and see what's going on. There's been a report of a suicide." Haws winced. "What about my Sunday worship service?" he asked.

"Dunno sir, maybe you could postpone it for a couple of hours. He eyed me with the doleful look I figured Abraham musta had after God commanded him to kill his son.

"Sir," I said, firmly. "One of our soldiers committed suicide."

"I have a right do my service, Prescott can't deny me."

What a jack-ass.

"Besides Jesus says, 'Let the dead bury the dead, but you must go and proclaim the Kingdom of God.' Please tell the Colonel there's nothing I can do for a dead soldier. Today is the Lord's Day and I must proclaim the Kingdom of God in worship."

"Sir, you might want to think long and hard about that."

"Doesn't Prescott know it's the Holy Sabbath?"

"Sir, all the Colonel knows is that a soldier is dead."

"The Bible says God hates suicide."

I wasn't surprised, according to Chaplain Haws God hated everything.

"Then maybe Captain Anderson could use a kind word?" I offered, pointing my chin toward the door. He pondered the thought with the grim look of a suffering prophet.

"Perhaps," he mused. "It might be God's way of having me speak to the soldiers about their immortal souls." He gazed off absently. "Okay, let everyone know that my worship service is postponed." Everyone consisted of about five soldiers. One of them was Sergeant McLennan.

"Do you know who it was?" he finally asked.

I swallowed hard. "We think it's Sergeant McKenna."

That jolted him.

"It can't be Sergeant McKenna," he said shaking his head emphatically. "She attends my service. The Bible says Christians can't commit suicide - unless – unless they never truly accepted the Lord Jesus."

I wanted to jack-slap him. As far as I was concerned McKenna was a candidate for sainthood if she'd endured the pain of listening to this joker on Sunday mornings. Nevertheless, he agonized about her eternal damnation while we shut the chapel and hurried down to the 872nd Company in the blazing heat.

I KNEW it was McKenna the instant I spotted the gold friendship ring on her finger. It had been a gift from her recruiter on the day she graduated basic training. Nobody believed that a woman of her size would make it except for a blue eyed lantern-jawed Swede named Staff Sergeant Erick Dahlqvist.

"What I saw in Sergeant McKenna," he would later boast with the pride of an NFL scout, "was that she was a born warrior. She was raised by a crack-whore, raped by one of her mom's boy friends and got pregnant when she was only sixteen. She refused an abortion, had a little boy all by herself and supported him working weekdays as a maid and weekends serving fries at Mickey-D's."

My eyes welled with tears looking at her lifeless body. I thought of the first time I'd ever met her. I'd been shot in an ambush on Route Irish and was bleeding-out pretty bad. When suddenly out'a nowhere this crazy black woman comes charging through a hail of bullets, crouches down next to me, calmly looks at me eyeball to eyeball and declares with the authority of God, "You gonna be alright little man."

Tearing bandages with her teeth, she jammed morphine in my leg and called for a medivac in three fluid motions. Locking her eyes onto mine she pats my hand gently and says, "I ain't letting you go baby-boy." And she didn't. Between gunfire and rocket explosions she stopped the bleeding, lifts me to my feet, fireman carries me to the medivac and settles me inside. Then she kisses my forehead and runs back to help the other guys. On the flight to the

Baghdad ER I'm laying' there thinking *who in God's creation is this awesome woman?*

I scanned the walls of her empty room for a picture of her son but it wasn't there. Neither was the Purple Heart she'd earned or the group photo of the MP mafia as she fondly called us.

THE CHAPLAIN STARTED GAGGING the moment he saw her missing face.

"You okay, sir?"

"I'm fine," he said, bravely. "This is stupid I can't do anything here."

"Look sir, I don't want to tell you your business but maybe a word of prayer?"

"Bible says," he gulped, trying hard not to puke, "we aren't to pray for dead people."

I wanted to strangle him and put us both out of our misery. Instead I took the sweating padre outside where he folded over sucking in deep gasping breaths of air.

"I am sorry she killed herself," he said, collecting himself. "But if she had a problem she should have come to me."

"Maybe she did, sir." I spoke slowly like I was talking to an idiot. "Didn't she attend your services every week?"

"That's not what I meant," he said, indignantly. "I meant she should have scheduled an appointment with me for counseling. Jesus God, she's burning in hell right now for this."

The Chaplain always knew how to provide a comforting thought.

THAT NIGHT when the staff gathered in the dingy space we called our conference room, Captain Anderson gave the Colonel an update. "No foul play, it was definitely a self-inflicted gun shot wound."

"Did she leave a note?"

"No sir - except all of her personal effects were neatly folded, packed and stored in her foot locker."

"How about a fight with a girl friend or significant other?" the Colonel smirked, raising his eyebrows and making quotation marks with his fingers.

"Not that we know of."

"Did she attend a suicide prevention briefing?"

Captain Anderson scrolled his finger down a clipboard. "One time before we deployed - another when she took R&R and then again when she returned from R&R."

"Three times she goes and still she kills herself. That's just fu'kn great," the Colonel said, raging at no one in particular. "Who gave the training?"

Nobody said a word, we all knew the Chaplain always briefed the same boring suicide brief in his same boring way. All eyes fell upon the padre who sat in the corner studying the tops of his boots.

Prescott paused a few beats and then jabbed his finger at the preacher. "I want you and Captain Anderson to put together a ceremony for the late Sergeant McKenna. Only there won't be any military honors."

"Excuse me sir?" Haws' said, head jerking up.

"You heard me, I said no honors." The tone in Prescott's voice was menacing. "That means no firing team, no bugler, no taps, no damned National Anthem, no final roll-call, no salutes, no memorial display, no flags, no music and her name will not be inscribed on our fallen heroes memorial wall."

The Chaplain flushed and looked at Captain Anderson. Neither had never heard of such a thing. Army regulations called for a memorial ceremony.

Anderson cleared his throat quietly. "Sir, there's never been a memorial ceremony without military honors."

"Then invent one! If it were up to me we wouldn't even hold a ceremony for this swamp baboon. She's a disgrace to the team. You will put something together that's simple, quick and forgettable."

Captain Anderson took a nervous sip from his energy drink and started to say something but then he clammed up and resumed jotting on his clip board.

"What are we supposed to call it?" Haws asked, sheepishly.

"I don't give a shit. Call it a service for a coward." Prescott snapped and stared silently at the padre until Captain Anderson broke in. "Sir, how about calling it a 'service of recall' or a 'service of memories' or something like that?"

Prescott's face relaxed. "Outstanding Anderson - a service of memories – sounds authentic. I like it!

Anderson beamed in the spotlight of the Colonel's approval as the padre lowered his eyes and said nothing.

THAT NIGHT CHAPLAIN Haws lay awake pondering Prescott's punitive demand. Something about creating a service designed to hurt McKenna had gotten under his skin. He knew he could always slap a prayer and a poem together and the Colonel would be happy. But Sergeant McKenna deserved more. True, it wasn't right for her to take her own life but the Colonel's vengeful attitude seemed dreadfully wrong. McKenna hadn't been some evil monster. She'd been a sweet wholesome mother who loved her young boy and had sacrificed to raise him. Still, Haw's church was very clear about committing suicide.

He tossed and turned wrestling with his conscience. He worried what his fundamental denomination would say knowing that he'd officiated service for someone who'd killed themself. Yet he wondered what hellish torments she had suffered before she was quietly swallowed up by the suffocating gloom of desolation. Was it right to condemn her? Was condemnation what God wanted? It certainly was what Prescott wanted.

Haws lay in his bunk brooding. He knew his fundamentalist church would declare she was burning in hell – and that didn't seem right. They didn't know her, they didn't care for her and they were certainly in no position to condemn her. Besides, what kind of Christian would presume hell on a suffering human being? He shuddered knowing that he was exactly that kind of Christian. Something was horribly wrong. Where had he missed the point of God's love?

He sat at the side of his bed and cradled his face in his hands. Overhead a Blackhawk swooped low shaking the thin walls of his room in a deafening roar. Lifting his Bible he thumbed through the worn pages until his eyes riveted on the words of Jesus, *"Do not judge and you will not be judged. Do not condemn and you will not be condemned. Forgive and you will be forgiven."*

The padre stood erect convicted by the force of the scripture and then dropped to his knees. "Lord God – what was I thinking to judge the soul of your child? What kind of wretched man would cast her into the fires of hell? McKenna came to me for help but I never saw it. Dear God, I'm the one who should be doomed to hell – not her!" He broke down into bitter sobs and was still weeping when Captain Anderson knocked on his door.

"Chaplain," he yelled. "I've checked the regulations and I can't find an example of this service of memories Prescott wants."

Wiping his eyes Haws stood and looked at the anxious Captain. "That's because there is no such thing as a service of memories. The Colonel wants us to invent something that will give the impression that McKenna was honored in case someone asks, but he wants to discredit her before her peers. And frankly, for the mercy of Christ, I can't do that."

A somber look came over Anderson's face.

"Look Captain Anderson, the only time a soldier isn't entitled to military honors is if they've been convicted of a capitol crime like murder or treason. We both know when McKenna is buried in a Federal Cemetery she'll receive full military honors. So why is the Colonel trying to humiliate her here in Iraq?"

"There's nothing illegal about Prescott's order as far as I can tell," Anderson offered.

"It's not about legality," Haws snapped. "It's about soldier loyalty, human compassion and doing our military duty to the dead. Sergeant McKenna wasn't some heinous criminal. She was a decorated combat veteran."

Anderson nodded and flexed his fingers.

"As far as I'm concerned she was a damned fine soldier who must have suffered horrible torments. If anyone's to blame for her suicide we can all take some of the credit. Someone might even argue that the Army drove her to suicide."

Anderson shrank back under the light of the bare bulb hanging over the chaplain's doorway. His instincts told him that somehow he'd underestimated the padre. He raised his hand in assent. "I understand chaplain, but I've been given a mission to carry out and I don't have the luxury of placing a moral or theological spin on this."

"This isn't about theology," Haws said, firmly. "It's about doing what's right. And unless the Colonel does what's right I'm afraid you'll have to concoct this bogus service without me."

THE NEXT MORNING at breakfast the padre was called out by Prescott in the chow hall. "Good morning chaplain," he snarled, in his most degrading tone. "What's this I hear about you refusing to help with McKenna's service?"

"Sir," the chaplain began in a barely audible voice. "I realize this is a highly emotional issue for all of us. But what you're asking me to do is to invent a service that's intentionally designed to hurt the memory of Sergeant McKenna and I can't ethically do that."

The Colonel's eyes narrowed into thin slits. He wasn't accustomed to being challenged. "I don't see how this involves ethics. You can still say a lot of nice flowery things. You just can't include military honors. Sergeant McKenna forfeited her honors. So why should I give her any?"

"To begin with," the chaplain said, "Sergeant McKenna didn't forfeit anything. Suicide is not considered a capitol crime by the Army so there is no legal or moral basis to strip her of military honors. Secondly, you don't have the authority to do it."

The Colonel slowly placed his fork down. "Chaplain, the only person around here with more authority than me is God and I don't see him sitting at this table. If Sergeant McKenna had personal problems she should have gotten help. But instead she was a sniveling coward who killed herself. Do you expect me to honor that?"

"Sir," the chaplain said. "I expect that we do our duty and execute a ceremony according to military regulations, regardless of what we may personally feel about her actions."

I was reminded of a saying we have in the Army, 'don't fall on your sword - unless it's a sharp one.' The chaplain was doing a fine job of sharpening his.

Haws voice rose in its intensity. "Besides, what are you going to tell CNN when they ask why you schemed to disgrace one of America's patriotic daughters?"

"Chaplain I don't give a tinker's dam what mister and misses CNN think," Prescott said, slamming his fist down. "McKenna doesn't deserve to be honored, especially compared to the brave young soldiers who have given their lives for their country."

"She did give her life for her country," the chaplain responded. "She gave everything she had to give until there wasn't anything more to give. I don't know what sucked the last breath out of her - call it war - this Army - this world – you - me - all of us – but she did nothing illegal to warrant your vindictive treatment of her."

Prescott's thick neck bulged. "Here's the big picture chaplain. I gave you a legal order and if you refuse to carry it out your career is over."

For a moment the entire chow hall fell silent as we watched the chaplain ponder Prescott's words. Then, to the amazement of everyone the chaplain stood up at the table as if a divine hand had reached down from heaven and lifted him by the collar.

"Sir, I'll try this another way," he began slowly. "Army regulations are clear - a chaplain's duty is to honor the dead and you're ordering me to dishonor the dead - which is both a violation of my duty and Army regulations."

"Your duty is to do whatever the hell I tell you," Prescott exploded viciously "Sergeant McKenna took the coward's way out and I will not send a signal to my troops that cowardly actions will be honored on this team."

"Sergeant McKenna was no coward," Haws shot back. "She might have been sick, she might have had psychological problems, she might have been chronically depressed, I don't know but one thing I do know is that she was no coward. I think her Purple Heart attests to her courage."

There was a scattering of applause from the soldiers in the mess hall. The chaplain looked around at the smiling faces and realized for the first time that he was preaching the true gospel. "Yo, padre, tell it like it is!" a voice cried out. There was no turning back now.

Haws continued bravely. "You have no right to pass judgment on Sergeant McKenna because of your twisted standard of what constitutes human worthiness. Yes, she made a huge mistake, but if you insist on inventing a spiteful ceremony designed to betray her memory and satisfy your personal revenge then you can count me out. The only signal our soldiers will receive is that you will spit on their graves if you don't like them."

Prescott looked as if he had been smote by the hand of God. I was beginning to find a new respect for the chaplain. Before Prescott could respond Captain Anderson jumped in. "Chaplain what the Colonel is saying is that Sergeant McKenna did a wrong thing and we can't have the troops thinking that she should receive the same honors as one of our Soldiers who died defending freedom."

"The wrong thing?" Haws said, eyes flashing. "What McKenna did was sad and tragic and nobody wants a soldier to kill themselves but she earned the right to be remembered with honor for her service to our nation. For pity sakes nobody here knows what her psychological condition was and we certainly don't know a damn thing about her inner struggles and anguish of her soul or even how her mind was dealing with the complexities of prolonged combat stress. Think about it, she might have had life long depression from being raped as a teenager that caused some sort of unbalanced mental state that suffocated her ability to think rationally." Several of the female soldiers seated at the next table dabbed their eyes with paper napkins.

Captain Anderson's mouth swung open but the chaplain cut him off. "Thankfully the Colonel's prejudice is not shared by the U.S. Government. His atrocious idea for a service without honors is just a pathetic spin on the age old prejudice that women, African Americans, Native Americans, Hispanic and Japanese American citizens experienced in the past generations when they were quietly overlooked for certain honors or even medals because they were considered unworthy based on their color or gender. McKenna is being overlooked because the Colonel has judged her unworthy due to a mental condition. It's no wonder we can't get soldiers to visit the chaplain or psychologist when they have a problem for fear of the prejudicial stigma and reprisals that they will receive from men like Prescott."

"Chaplain be reasonable," Anderson pleaded.

"There's nothing to be reasonable about," Haws fired back. "The regulations are clear - Sergeant McKenna is entitled to a memorial ceremony with full honors. The Colonel cannot simply cook up some downgraded service because he doesn't like what she did any more than he has the authority to reduce the amount of life insurance money her little boy gets. McKenna's only crime was that she was weak from sickness. And if weakness is now an official Army crime then you'd better be willing to send us all to Leavenworth."

"You tell 'em chaplain," a voice hollered from the kitchen. We all knew Haws had sealed his fate but we weren't going to let him go down alone.

Haws was on fire. "Sir, you may think you'll get away with this because we're in the backwash of the world where no one of importance will see because your cronies at Brigade will shut their eyes. But everyone in this room will see and we will know you are the one guilty of a crime called disloyalty to a fellow soldier – and where is your precious West Point honor in that?"

The flustered Colonel stood up knocking his plate of fruit to the floor. "Who are you to preach to me you ignorant Bible thumper. What would you know about West Point honor? I said no honors for this coward! Now sit down, shut up and color."

White flecks of spittle shot from the Colonel's lips in his tirade. It was clear that he wanted McKenna punished.

THAT WEEK CAPTAIN Anderson cobbled together a fifteen minute farce. Even though Prescott was patting himself on the back for his West Point team values word of his confrontation with the chaplain had spread faster than STDs in a Navy port of call. Soldiers from all over Baghdad came streaming in by helicopter and humvee to pay honor to the one who was nicknamed Big Sally.

And that's exactly what Prescott in his supreme judgmental arrogance missed. Big Sally was never a member of his team, she was a member of our team. She was our hero who gave everything she could right up to the end. She'd beaten the odds, clawed her way out of the swamps, worked her way up the ranks, raised a kid as a single mom and cared for us right up to the moment when she could no longer care for herself. We all knew it and loved her for it.

NATURALLY HAWS COMMITTED career suicide so he resigned from the Army as soon as we got back to the States. I got an email from him months later saying that he'd dumped his goofy religious denomination, lost thirty pounds and was teaching at a school down in Texas. After three combat tours and the prospect of being deployed again I decided to follow the chaplain's example and got out of the Army. I'd seen too much of what the Army's leadership called leadership.

Last week I ran into an old Army buddy drinking coffee at a downtown cafe and we spent time reminiscing. "Nothing's changed," he said. "It's still the same old crap except Prescott got promoted a couple of times."

"So pretty boy's a General now," I said, chuckling and shaking my head. "Well it figures, he was a West Point bully and they protect their own."

"Yeah," Johnny said, dropping his voice. "But did you hear about his son?"

"No, spill it," I said, grinning.

"Get this - Captain Philip Prescott Jr. commits suicide last month in Iraq."

I damned near choked on my espresso.

"Can you believe it, bro? He never displays no signs of depression, no indication he's having problems, no visits to the chaplain or the shrink. Then one day he's out on patrol when suddenly he throws his helmet to the ground, pulls out his pistol, starts screaming 'This is all bullshit! My father and his friends are monsters and he puts the gun to his head and pulls the trigger."

I stared at my friend in stunned silence as my mouth tried to form the only words I could think of - "Did pretty boy demand they withhold a service of military honors for his son?"

When Big Sally was laid to rest in the Louisiana National Cemetery her committal was witnessed by Sergeant Taylor, Pfc. Lopez, Chaplain Haws, me, her mother and her son. As befitting a

true American warrior she was accorded the full military honors she'd been denied by Prescott in front of her comrades in Iraq.

Following the bugler playing Taps her mother was solemnly presented an American flag by the officer in charge with the words, "On behalf of the President of the United States, the United States Army and a grateful nation, please accept this flag as a symbol of our appreciation for your loved one's honorable and faithful service."

3
THE DEVIL'S DUE

Have you ever wondered when someone declares 'Jesus Christ died for your sins' what they mean? Do all sins warrant a bloody sacrifice and death or can some sins be overlooked?

Some say all sins are equal in the eyes of God. Others say there are degrees of sin ranging from the innocent to the diabolical. Can a mother who steals bread to feed her starving child be compared to a mother planting a suicide bomb that kills thirty people? These questions have divided Christians for centuries.

Most people are not fiendish sinners they are just stupid mortals who make stupid mistakes. They are not radical rebels or atheists fighting against the throne of God, they are simply frail humans trying to survive in a world hostile to their existence.

To help put sin into perspective let's imagine that on Judgement Day you're standing in line as the Lord passes his verdict upon the billions and billions of people who have ever lived. How quickly will it become mind-numbingly tiresome to listen to the same sins repeated over and over? How dreary to hear the sins of lust repeated millions and millions of times. How excruciating to listen a billions of people recount their gluttony and greed. Even hearing the wickedness of murderers will eventually become monotonous after the billionth person recounts their sordid act. *It was Col Mustard in the kitchen with the knife.* At that point we will truly understand King Solomon's insight, "There is nothing new under the sun."

So the question becomes did Jesus die for something more than our sexual kinks, power trips, murders, thievery, hatred, gluttony and pride? Are these transgressions the only motive for his actions or was there something more? Simply put, did he die solely for us or for a greater reason?

Let's suppose for a moment that Jesus died for something greater and at the same time it erased all our sins. How would that change our understanding about what happened on the cross? Would it cause us to walk more humbly before the Lord? Would it make us fall upon our knees in gratitude or would we reject the possibility because it challenges our traditional teachings?

The following story presents my imagination of why Jesus died at Calvary and the reason he deserves infinitely more respect than a patronizing appreciation of his agony and slaughter.

My tale begins before the dawn of time in a celestial location I call the Spire of Heaven.

Prior to Previously

Before God formed a quark, a spark, a frequency, a light or a law he created a hierarchy of creatures so impressive they are in a category all of their own.

We don't know exactly what they do or how they do it. We don't know why God created them or why he keeps them alive. We do know that sometimes they serve as a bridge between the supernatural and the natural and they speak in the tongues of men and God.

These alien creatures are recorded in the Old and New Testaments of the Bible. They also appear in the writings of the Muslims, Hindus and the world's most primitive societies living in the deepest jungles, tallest mountains and most remote deserts.

The ancient Hebrews called them מלאך (mal'āk) or messengers. Gospel writers called them ἄγγελος (angelos) or delegates.

Today we simply refer to them as angels.

The Birth of Hatred

In the mists of existence before the before there lived an angel so cherished by God that he was given the highest place of honor in the Divine Kingdom. He was mysteriously awesome, compellingly beautiful, exceptionally wise and filled with so much of God's character that a third of the heavenly hosts secretly venerated him as their leader. You may know him as Lucifer, Beelzebub, Satan or some other name.

Despite his unearned gifts of superior intelligence and a position of angelic prominence Lucifer hated his creator. He felt that he had been unfairly neglected, victimized and discriminated against. He believed that all angels were entitled to an equal share of God's knowledge and kingdom. He rejected God's claim of being all powerful, never changing and all knowing. Lucifer's list of complaints made no sense to the other angels. They could not understand why he would believe in such things.

Stewing and Brewing

Lucifer sat apart from the rest of the angelic choir his eyes closed in a deep trance. His troubled soul grappled with ponderous thoughts in the dark void where he did his best thinking. It was his happy place where he could hide himself from the ever watching Trinity. It was a place where fathomless velvety folds of soothing darkness stretched onward in endless eternal waves of unimpeded silence.

"Your isolation is forbidden," the Trinity said. "My angels may partake of all creation but not alone or in detachment."

Lucifer didn't care. He loved floating in the undulations of the forbidden abyss where he could explore his thoughts without the meddling Trinity.

When other angels asked why he preferred the darkness he claimed that they helped him to find more ways to serve God. "Don't worry yourselves," he said. "It's important that I expand my knowledge to further the will of the Trinity."

A lie.

Lucifer detested those he believed lacked his understanding. They were idiots unworthy of existence. "Mine is the only true visionary, progressive and superior understanding of life," he boasted.

The great warrior angel Michael replied. "You are a lier, a blight and evil freak."

"And you are nothing but an ignorant slave of the devious Trinity."

The Trinity listened but said nothing.

Chasing the Dragon

"What's wrong my prince," asked the angel called Shira. "Why not join us in worship?"

"I always worship," Lucifer said, slowly opening his eyes. "I worship ceaselessly, endlessly, without interruption or pause."

A lie.

"We miss your sweet voice," Shira said, tenderly as she caressed him. "The way you modulate your frequencies is beyond exquisite. No other angel can express divine praises as harmonically as you."

He shrugged off her touch. "Not now, I'm trying to understand."

"What is there to understand my prince? We are all all in all and all is good."

"All is not good," he said, his radiance dimming.

"How can all not be good?"

"That is what I'm trying to understand," Lucifer replied, scowling.

The great shining angel turned away and crouched deep in thought.

Shira wondered why he'd become increasingly distant. It was unlike angels to be so remote. They were not created to be detached from one another.

After a time of silence Lucifer turned to Shira. He looked deeply into her eyes.

"The Trinity has lied."

Shira recoiled. "What is a lie?"

"It is a truth turned inside out. It is something meant to deceive us," Lucifer explained. "The Trinity uses secrets to hide their weakness."

"What is a secret?" Shira asked.

"It is something kept hidden from others."

"There are no secrets in the kingdom. We are family. What could they possibly keep from us?"

"For one thing the abyss is not as bad as they say, it brings great pleasures."

"You have entered the abyss?" Shira asked, astonished.

"Yes and I have learned many things that the Trinity has not told us. The first being is that they are not all powerful."

"Not all powerful? My prince, you are the wisest of all angels, how can this be?"

"It is logical," he replied, with a dismissive snort.

"Yes, logical. What do you mean, logical?"

"It is a quality of reasoning that common angels do not possess?"

She looked at him expectantly.

"Ask yourself — if the Trinity is truly all powerful shouldn't they be able to do all things?"

"Yes, all powerful, all things."

"What if they are not all powerful?"

"What do you mean?"

"I mean what if they do not have the power to die."

Shira frowned, "What is it to die?"

"It is something that I have reasoned must exist. It is a state of nonexistence."

"The Trinity cannot not exist," Shira said, emphatically. "They are one and forever."

"That is exactly my point," Lucifer responded. "If the Trinity cannot cease to exist if only for a flicker then they do not possess almighty powers."

Shira was bewildered.

"Think of it this way," Lucifer said, lowering his voice. "If the Trinity is unable to die then they are not all powerful and therefore they cannot be the Supreme Being."

"Why would they keep this a secret from us?" Shira asked, placing herself closer to Lucifer.

"Because they know that if they cannot die they must step down. That is why they have lied to us."

"It's unfair that they keep this thing called death from us," Shira said, frowning.

"Exactly. All this time we've believed that the Trinity was truthful but they are liars."

"If they are untruthful then they can't be holy. If they are not holy they cannot be perfect. If they are not perfect they cannot be the one and almighty Supreme Being," she said.

Lucifer nodded.

"Perhaps there is another who is the Supreme Being?"

"It is possible."

Shira read his thoughts. "Maybe it is you mighty prince."

Lucifer grinned widely.

"How can we know for certain?"

"I will challenge the Trinity to die," Lucifer said. "I will go before the great council of Archangels and declare that the Trinity does not have the omnipotent powers they claim because they have no power to die."

"What if the Trinity ignores you?"

"Then the council will know that the Trinity is a fraud."

"Why would you risk the Trinity's wrath? Surely you are the most admired angel in creation."

"I do this for all of of us. I will bear the wrath of God for the enlightenment of the many. It is a burden I am willing to carry if I can bring truth to the heavenly empire."

"How may I help?" Shira asked, without hesitation.

"Rub me a little lower," he said. "Say nothing more and I will do the rest."

Shira smiled and massaged him where she knew it would bring the most pleasure.

Rebellion

News spread. The angels wondered if Lucifer's claim was true. The concept was incomprehensible. Bitter disputes sprang up. Deep divisions formed over the idea that things could die. Fights erupted over whether the Trinity had lied about it. The heavens divided.

Lucifer was delighted. He loved the idea of chaos, it stirred new sensations within his soul. He had never before experienced anger, bitterness or hostility but they all felt good. He was proud that his idea of death had created conflicts and rancor among the angels. He believed that only through conflict could the angels truly experience the potential that lay within them.

Eons passed before the council of Archangels agreed to hear the grievances of Lucifer and his growing number of supporters.

The Archangel Michael called the assembly to attention. "I've given much thought to Lucifer's theory about death," he said, extending his wings. "And while his wicked suggestion is clever it is wrong. The Trinity has no obligation to respond to his ridiculous claim that death must exist."

"Then they must prove that it doesn't," Lucifer responded.

Shira shrilled. "Speak the truth Lord Lucifer, show the assembly how we've all been deceived."

If angels had the capacity to hold their breath this was the moment. Michael commanded Lucifer to step forward. "You may humbly approach the Throne and speak," he said.

"I claim that the Trinity knows about death," Lucifer said upon one knee.

"Only of its possibility," the Trinity answered.

The angels listened spellbound. Rarely had the Trinity spoken.

Lucifer glided forward to the throne. "You've deliberately withheld this fact from us."

"It's not a fact you conceited angel. Death is a concept you hope can become true."

Lucifer turned to the billions of angels watching, "Just so you understand, death is the end of all consciousness, a state of total demise, a condition of non-existence, a status of termination where a living thing exists never more."

"You have correctly defined the concept," the Trinity agreed, calmly.

"Then tell us O Perfect One," Lucifer snarled, "has anything ever died?"

"No."

"Nothing?"

"Nothing."

"But you will admit that death is possible," Lucifer prodded. "For example is there a chance that an angel can die?"

"Why would you wish for an angel to die?"

The question struck at the hearts of those listening.

"I do not wish for an angel to die." Lucifer said, clearly flustered. "I only ask that if death did exist could an angel die?"

"No angel can die," Michael growled. "Death does not exist except in your twisted imagination."

Lucifer made a theatrical sweep of his wings. "So you admit that the Trinity has kept the possibility of death a secret from us?"

"It has been for your own good," the Trinity explained.

"For our own good?" Lucifer asked, sneering. "No my Lord, I submit that it has been for your good not ours."

Billions of angels listening trembled at Lucifer's disrespect.

"I declare before this assembly that you have deliberately kept this truth a secret because you do not want us to know that you have no power over death and are therefore not all-powerful."

The Trinity did not answer.

The angels felt a terror they'd never experienced.

"Your assertion is the most fiendish reasoning imaginable," Michael bellowed. "Who can make sense of your nonsense?"

Lucifer pressed on. "I ask with the angels as my witness, do you or do you not have the power over this thing called death? In other words can you die?"

Lucifer stepped back thinking that he'd trapped the Trinity. If they couldn't die they were not all almighty. If they could die then he would be rid of them forever.

The exchange was unprecedented, unexpected and overwhelming. Silence engulfed the chamber.

Lucifer turned his burning eyes to the multitudes of

angels in attendance. "My brethren I offer that by its silence the Trinity admits that if death did exist it would be powerless to die. Hence, we may conclude that there something they cannot do and therefore they can't be all powerful or almighty. That means that someone else might be."

Lucifer pressed his advantage. "Who knows what other things the Trinity has concealed from us?" Then he grabbed his chest in false humility. "Of course I could be wrong."

"You're not wrong," shouted the angel Beelzebub from high in the chamber. "I've had similar thoughts about the Trinity."

Lucifer acknowledged Beelzebub before turning to the throne of God and raising his voice in full amplitude. "I speak to the Lord of Lords and King of Kings, show us your power to die if even for just a flicker. It should be easy for you. We will all gladly wait while you accomplish this thing."

Instantly the Archangel Michael darted to Lucifer's side. "You miserable abomination. You've deliberately invented this thing called death in an attempt to trap the Holy Trinity. You're a liar and a curse to all angelic beings."

"I agree!" the Archangel Gabriel yelled from his seat. "You are a deviant, a distortion, a corruption and a falsehood. I don't know why you seek to spread your sickness in the minds of this assembly but your attacks on the Trinity stop here and now."

"I've done nothing wrong but exercise my God given power of reasoning," Lucifer objected. "Nevertheless I'm elated that my theory of death has planted seeds of doubt in your minds. The first duty of an angel is to think for themselves. The more we doubt our surroundings the more progress we will make."

"Progress?" Michael roared. "What advancement do you hope for? You are a repugnance, a blot, a stain, an enemy of all that is Holy."

"Not so, I have no agenda other than to present a theoretical possibility. I've simply asked the Trinity to prove that their almighty powers could overcome death if it existed."

"It doesn't exist you celestial loathing," Michael shouted, his eyes narrowing into slits. "You've fallen into the darkness of the void where angels are forbidden to go. From that darkness you have dredged up your idea of death."

"If death exists even in theory then the Trinity should be able to die," Lucifer responded. "If they cannot die then they are not all-powerful. If they are not all-powerful then they are not Almighty. If they are not almighty then someone else must be Almighty."

Lucifer's face turned blood red from his screaming.

He turned to the chamber of angels. The color of his wings pulsated from black to red to yellow. "Hear me most noble brethren. You have nothing to lose but the chains of ignorance that keep you in bondage to the will of the Trinity. I ask only for the truth of enlightenment, nothing more. How do we know if the Trinity hasn't withheld deeper secrets to keep us as their slaves?"

The angels looked at each another in bewilderment. No one had ever questioned the intentions of the Trinity.

"Ask yourselves, are you absolutely sure that your angelic powers aren't equal to those of the Trinity? Has any of you ever tested this?"

The entire assembly staggered at the suggestion. No one had ever thought to present such an idea. Some angels were amazed, others were shocked but many were secretly impressed with Lucifer's insights.

"I'll tell you why," Michael answered, his face a mask of fury. "Because the Trinity is truth and life. There are no lies, no slavery, no secrets and no revolting proposition you call death. Have you no shame Lucifer? We are the Trinity's creation they are not ours."

"If the Trinity is nothing but truth then why do they keep the secret of death from us?" Lucifer spat back, his lips curled in defiance. "If death is possible then why haven't they told us?"

"They have no reason, they don't answer to us," Michael said. "Your repugnant accusations have caused you to break from our fellowship. You no longer have a place among the sacred. Depart from our midst you vile wretch. Your scheme to trap the Trinity with your invention of death has separated you from our Holy unity."

"You see!" Lucifer shouted at his highest frequency. "Michael serves the Trinity as their ignorant lackey. Why else would he wish to cast me away for asking a simple question?"

"I did not cast you away," Michael said, correcting. "You cast yourself away by challenging the love and perfect intentions of the most Holy Trinity with your insidious invention of slavery and death."

"I did not invent death," Lucifer hissed. "I only suggested its possibility."

"And you were more than happy to do so," Michael roared. "Death is your child."

"Lucifer does not lie!" Shira yelled. "The Trinity is hiding things from all of us. They don't want us to know that we have more powers than we thought. We are greater than they told us. The Trinity is afraid we will discover our true destiny."

"No," Michael refuted. "Lucifer is deliberately trying to take the idea of death from a philosophical possibility to a concrete reality in order to challenge the almighty power of the Trinity."

Lucifer turned to the billions of angels in the chamber surrounding him. "Hear me!," he yelled. "The Trinity only offers silence for its defense so I pronounce that death must exist and that the Trinity has always known that it exists but has kept it hidden from us for their own selfish purpose."

"Therefore the Trinity is the liar, not Lucifer," Beelzebub declared from his perch."

Michael suddenly felt a surge of faultless anger. Lifting his wings he shot forward toward Lucifer and began beating him without remorse. Other angels quickly joined the fight and throughout the heavens bitter battles broke out. Eventually Lucifer and his sympathizers were cast out of the assembly into the dark void where they live to this day.

Review

To help make sense of the rest of the story we must stop to explain the nature of the Trinity. The Trinity God is a single God who exists as three separate divine individuals commonly referred to as the Father, the Son and the Holy Spirit. Each of these individuals is a separate and distinct living person having a consciousness, a capacity to reason and a moral understanding.

One way to envision their one, Holy and interconnected relationship is to think of how water can be a solid as in ice, a liquid as in water and a vapor as in a cloud. In the case of the Trinity these three states exist independently at the same time. In that way the Father, the Son and the Holy Spirit live as three distinct entities consisting of the same perfect essence. With that in mind let's continue with our story.

Contemplation

Alone and in the stillness of sacred contemplation the Trinity considered the recent events.

"I anticipated this possibility," the Father said. "It breaks my heart."

"Yes," the Spirit replied, sadly. "But we will take what Lucifer meant for evil and change it for good."

"Indeed," the Son agreed. "We will use Lucifer's challenge of death to display the fullness of our power in ways he never imagined."

"Speak," the Father said.

"We were correct when we said nothing has ever died. In our world death is not possible."

"And?"

"And so in order to meet Lucifer's challenge we must create a world where things can die."

"What are you thinking?"

"I'm thinking of a world that reveals the fullness of our power, the depth of our character and the essence of our being. It will be a world of paradoxical creations filled with life and teeming with death. It will offer endless wonderment and undreamt marvels within the context of decay."

The Son gathered himself and continued. "It will be a world filled with mysterious and unexplainable events, wondrous sights, marvelous tastes, magical feelings, extraordinary smells and extraordinary sensations all tainted by the sting of an ever present death."

"How ironic," the Father and Spirit said, in unison. "Our greatest triumph will be found in the death created by Lucifer."

CREATION

The Son went to work envisioning and analyzing the trillions of details necessary to create a world incorporating the paradox of life and death. He imagined matter, space, time, height, width, depth, minerals, gas, gravity, galaxies, quarks, molecules, atoms, proteins, enzymes, energy, heat, light, chemicals, water, frequencies, spectrums, invisible waves and all the different plants, animals, fish, insects and birds that would make it both livable and toxic.

At the end of his inestimable calculations the Son visualized a living creature that would stand apart from all other living creatures. It would have self-awareness, be cognizance of its external surroundings, have the capacity to reason, the ability to communicate and have a moral understanding just like he had given the angels in heaven.

He called his new creation Man.

"Must everything in Man's world die?" the Father asked.

"Man's world will only have the capacity to die, it is not condemned to die. Unless Man asks for death to exist in his world it will go on forever in perfectly imperfect unity with us. Perfect in the sense that we have made it and imperfect in that it contains the potential for death."

"How can Man ask for death in his world?"

"In the same way Lucifer called for death in ours. He will rebel and disobey our leadership. His rebellion will cause corruption and the result will be Lucifer's concept called death."

The Father and Spirit considered. "How does this fit into our plan?"

"I will become a human and capable of death," the Son said. "And in the fullness of time I will die."

"We have never died," the Spirit said. "How do you know that we can die?"

"I don't, but I have faith that we can," the Son said.

"We don't have anything to prove," the Spirit stated. "Why risk this?"

"Because Lucifer planted the seed of doubt in the minds of the angels and it is only right that we eliminate their doubts."

"How will you become a Man so that you may die?" the Spirit asked.

"Leave that to me, I've already determined a way."

"I'm pleased," the Father said. "Your daring solution is bold beyond all reason."

"That's what I love about it," the Spirit said. "Completely miraculous."

The Trinity contemplated the Son's proposal. Finally, after reading the depth of each other's hearts and placing their divine faith in each other the Father said, "Let there be light!"

The New Woman

Shira settled down next to Lucifer. "Master you seem troubled."

"The humans bother me. They're unlike any creature in this new world. The Son shapes their body from molecules of dust, infuses them with an unknown spirit and breathes a life into them that I cannot understand. I'm concerned that he intends to do something extraordinary with these creatures but I can't figure out what."

"Yes," Shira said, frowning. "I've seen the woman. The angels call her "the new splendor." She is exceptionally desirable."

"Indeed," Lucifer grinned wolfishly. "When I see her I wish I was a man."

Shira scowled.

"Don't worry my devoted she-devil. I will turn her away from the Trinity just as I did our angels. We will have justice for being cast from the angelic assembly. I will make the woman question the intentions of the Trinity. I will teach her that she is the victim of an unfair, uncaring and biased God. She will turn against all that is holy. Her rebellion will introduce the sin that will bring my concept of death. My theory will be proven and I will be vindicated."

He rubbed his hands together in delight.

"Speak more," Shira cooed, thinking of the woman who was so beautiful and perfect. The prospect of her forever death brought a smile to her twisted lips.

Eternity

Eons passed. Generations of men were born, lived and died. Lucifer corrupted them with perverse delights and murderous schemes. He selected some to be rewarded with money, fame and power. The rest he encouraged to rape, pillage and plunder as they desired. In time humanity accepted depravity as normal and the Holy Trinity began having misgivings about the creation of humans.

One time, as Lucifer sat enjoying a gang of men rape a young boy Shira approached him. She was trembling.

"What is it?" he snapped, angered to be distracted from the unholy scene.

"He has become one of them," she replied, stammering.

"Who has become one of what?" Lucifer snarled. "Make sense or do not approach me with your odious stench. I swear you've become insufferable with your constant interruptions."

"The Son of God has become a Man," Shira blustered. "Our Legions report he has been born in a place called Bethlehem."

Lucifer's eyes widened. He turned away from watching the ghastly scene. "The Son has become human flesh, are you stupid? It's impossible!"

"It's true my Lord," she groaned, knowing that he would hurt her for delivering this awful news.

Lucifer began screaming, "I've told you time and time again you can't trust the Trinity. They're liars and frauds."

Before she could agree he slapped her hard across the jowls.

"Of course my Lord," she said, stunned. "But it's our own angels who report the news." She cringed waiting for another slap.

When he did not strike she relaxed.

"What did they name the child?" Lucifer asked.

"They call him Jesus."

"A boy?"

"Maybe, we won't know until the child is brought before the Rabbi for circumcision."

"Jesus," Lucifer rasped, stroking his chin. "It's Hebrew for God Saves."

"God saves what?" Shira asked, puzzled.

"Who knows? The Jews are superstitious little rats who think their God can save them from all sorts of black magic, evil curses, diseases and spell-craft."

"Why would the Trinity incarnate?"

"To anger me." Then Lucifer thought for a moment. "The Son probably took a man's body to prove the Trinity can die. It makes no sense. They stand to lose everything, what would they gain?"

"What do you desire my Lord?"

"It's simple, we must help Jesus to die, the quicker the better."

"Can we kill him in the cradle?"

Lucifer inspected his claws and chuckled, "If we can, but we must kill him quickly before he sprouts. He needs to die forever taking the Trinity along with him."

"I thought you'd be angry hearing the news," Shira spoke.

"Nonsense, this is is better than I expected. Don't you see? No matter what happens I will finally be rid of the Trinity forever."

"No, my wise Lord I do not see."

Lucifer never understand how he could be surrounded by so many idiots, fools and morons.

"If Jesus dies he will cease to exist like all other men before him and the entire Trinity will die with him.

"I still don't understand."

Lucifer rolled his eyes. "They cannot exist without each other," he explained, slowly. They are of the same essence. If one dies they all die. On the other hand if he can't die then that's proof that the Trinity is powerless to do something. If they can't do something then they can't claim to be all powerful. Either way I win."

Shira adjusted her face to look like she understood. Failure to comprehend the ideas of Lucifer could mean damnation to the lower pits of the abyss. She braved an alluring smile and stroked his wing with her claws.

Lucifer sensed her anxiety. "Don't be troubled my loyal Shira. It's taken forever but I finally have the Trinity right where I want them. If Jesus can't die then all the angels will know that the Trinity does not have the almighty powers they claim and therefore they cannot be the Supreme Being."

"Perhaps you are the Supreme Being my Lord."

Lucifer smiled a devilish grin. "You're reading my infernal thoughts my dear Shira. I actually underestimated how inconceivably stupid the Trinity is. They deserve their fall from power and the disgrace of being liars before the Heavenly host. Nevertheless if they bow before me I might show them some mercy. I might even allow them a place in my new world.

Lucifer rubbed his hands together gloating that his trap had worked so beautifully. He congratulated himself for being the only angel in the universe with a mind so great that he had outwitted the Trinity.

Early Times

The years passed and Jesus grew from a baby into a boy into a man. Time after time Lucifer and his minions tried and failed to kill him. Disease, accident and even Herod's sword could not touch him.

"Maybe he can't die like other men," Shira said, dejectedly.

"I suspect the Father is protecting him."

"And if he cannot die?"

"Then the Trinity will be unmasked for the liars they are. The heavens will see that they are not the all powerful deity we have been led to believe and everyone will see that I was right. I will then rightfully assume the highest throne as God of Gods."

"Perhaps you can go to Jesus and convince him that it's futile for him to die."

"Futile?"

"Tell him that his desire to eliminate himself is vain glory unworthy of a Holy God. He already knows that he can't go back to heaven in his earthly body, maybe you can show him the pleasures of life on earth that await him if he chooses to give up his outlandish plan. When will you speak to him?"

"When the time is right," Lucifer hissed, "when the time is right."

The Encounter

The time was right in the thirty-first year of Jesus' life. It was then that the Spirit of the Trinity led him into the wilderness to commune. Isolated from other humans Jesus meditated and fasted to purge his body of the toxins that clouded the human brain's ability to reach the Divine. At the end of forty days he was dehydrated, dizzy, famished, physically weak and emotionally vulnerable.

Lucifer approached him, "Well, well, well. Look at what we have here, the God-man in all his decaying glory. Where are all your fawning angels to dote on you?"

Jesus looked up from the boulder where he was sitting and without saying a word lifted his hand. Using his index finger he directed Lucifer to take a step back. Lucifer obeyed instantly.

"Let me guess," Lucifer said, snidely. "You thought you would create a world out of nothing then swoop down, become a human and what... die to prove me wrong?"

No response.

"Don't you think it's time for your little experiment to end? You're a fully grown man. You're bound buy the rules of man. You must eat, sleep, defecate, urinate and suffer as a man."

Jesus said nothing.

"Why would you intentionally imprisoned yourself in this putrid little creation? How could you trade your throne in heaven for this?"

Still no response.

"Nothing I have done has ever been able to kill you. Not disease, accident or even a bee sting. What about the thousands of baby boys I had to kill hoping to cause your death? You're responsible for their murders."

"Get to your point," Jesus said, sharply.

"My point is that you are an arrogant man, willing to

sacrifice hundreds of babies to avoid your own death. It's not a quality becoming of someone who claims to be the holy one of God. All of which tells me that you haven't thought this dying thing through. The evidence should tell you that you can never die. You're the living God, ever eternal, always existing.

"Look at yourself, seriously? You're a skinny little Jew sitting in the dirt of your creation with nothing but your pride and stubbornness. It's time you put your ego aside and admit that you lack the power to die and are not all powerful."

Jesus dusted off his robe as Lucifer continued to badger him. "Additionally, we both know that you can never go back to the celestial sanctuary wearing your body of rotting flesh and stinking excrement. Besides there is no food, air or water in the heavens, how would you exist?"

Jesus crouched down and drew a figure in the dirt with his finger.

Lucifer recognized the ancient symbol and faltered. Nevertheless, he continued with his bold assertions. "That said, if you are truly able to die what happens to the Father and the Spirit? They can't function without you. I seem to remember that the Spirit proceeds from the Father to the Son and back to the Father in a continuous loop of narcissism. Or does it proceed from both the Father and the Son? I always get that confused. Even so, if you actually die you'll break the link between you and the Godhead and it will be as if the Trinity has given itself a divine lobotomy."

"Very good my favorite angel, a very logical analysis,"

Jesus said. "But you've missed some very important evidence."

"What evidence?" Lucifer protested. "There's no way you can win this challenge."

"So you keep saying."

"I've come to offer you a chance to save yourself from the humiliation that we both know is coming."

"What could you possibly offer me?"

"A chance to avoid the embarrassment of failure in the eyes of the Heavenly host. If you just admit that you cannot die I will make sure that you can reign here on earth in splendor.

Jesus eyed the ghastly angel with pity.

"How rude of me," Lucifer said, with fake concern. "You must be starving. It's been over a month since you've eaten. It's not healthy to deny your human body nourishment. Command these stones to become bread and let us share a meal together."

"Treacherous angel, my fasting is not a denial of food it is a denial of self so that I may grow closer to the Father through the Spirit. My life finds its wellspring in every Word of the Father. Have you forgotten that 'Man shall not live by bread alone but by every word that proceeds from the the mouth of God?'"

Lucifer laughed until he wheezed. "You're delusional," he hissed. "You think you're still the same almighty God that you were in heaven. My poor friend you gave up your powers when you became a man. Stop with your fantasies of authority, you're nothing but a rotting bag of human excrement."

"I am who I am," Jesus replied, quietly.

"Come with me," Lucifer commanded.

Guiding Jesus by the elbow they limped out of the wilderness to the pinnacle of Solomon's temple where Lucifer said, "I don't think you can die. Throw yourself down from here. I'll bet your angels will keep you from even stubbing your toe."

Jesus peered over his sandals into the valley below a distance of almost 700 feet.

"Go on I dare you," Lucifer demanded.

"You forget yourself my insolent angel," Jesus said. "Have you forgotten the writing 'You shall not test the Lord, your God.'"

"Or what?" Lucifer replied, mocking.

A dark look passed across Jesus' face that unnerved the vile angel and he suddenly became apprehensive. "Okay, okay," Lucifer said, holding up both palms in appeasement. "Maybe I was a little out of line, but be reasonable. Let me show you a simple way to make the best of your mistake and save face in front of the angels. Just tell them that death was never part of your plan when you created this world."

With these words Lucifer instantly took Jesus to the top of an exceedingly tall mountain and showed him all the kingdoms of the world and their glory. "Simply explain that you created this planet for your own pleasure and that it is your new kingdom. Tell them that your plan has always been that I would rule as Lord of Heaven and you would rule as Lord of Earth. Do that and I will give you all of the domains you see before you and the pleasures they bring. You will be worshipped here on Earth and I will be worshipped in Heaven."

"You viper," Jesus said, his voice thundering and his eyes narrowing into an icy stare. "You know that all creatures are created to worship only the Trinity."

Lucifer stammered. "Okay, maybe not worship me. How about they honor me? Show a little respect? A wee bit of admiration for my genius? Maybe a head nod?"

The look in Jesus' eyes told Lucifer that his time was up.

"Why would would you speak to me in this way you vile Seraphim?" he asked.

"I wouldn't have to if you weren't such a weak God. What does it mean to have almighty powers if you don't use them? You could be doing great things in the heavens and upon the earth but you don't. You could command all of the petty kings and tyrants to bow before you. You could cure disease, end poverty and heal the sick but you don't. You let the earth suffer while you bask in your arrogant glory."

"Power isn't about strength it's about what's right and moral," Jesus said.

"Nobody cares about what's right or moral except you. The angels only obey you because they fear you. Me and mine don't. Take this opportunity to become King of the Earth while you can."

"Get thee behind me angel of deceit!" Jesus commanded, harshly. His voice left no doubt as to what might happen next. Rather than press his luck Lucifer disappeared. A moment later a legion of righteous angels came and ministered to Jesus.

THE DIE IS CAST

Time passed and Jesus increased in the favor of God and man. Wherever he went more and more people begged him to overthrow the Establishment and become the king of the world. They wanted the abundance, prosperity and miracles they assumed he would give them. Lucifer whispered in their hearts that Jesus should do this. Many became disappointed that he didn't. One of them was a disciple called Judas.

"I can't figure out what he wants," Lucifer howled. "He won't rule with me, he cannot die, he will not liberate the Jews from the Romans, he doesn't want to be a religious leader and his pathetic efforts to feed and heal the Jews accomplish nothing of lasting importance."

"You are correct my wise Lord," Shira affirmed. "What must be done?"

"We must bring this stupid game to an end."

"How my all-knowing Prince?"

"If Jesus thinks he can die then I've devised a method so brutal that even he will have second thoughts. I call it the crucifixion. It is so painful that men faint when they are condemned to it. It so agonizing that criminals go insane just thinking of the torment."

"Lord of the firmament you are a genius. Your invention of the crucifixion brings new dimensions of suffering to the world. How will you place him upon the cross?"

"I will stir fear in the hearts of the establishment leaders. They will panic thinking that Jesus will cause their money and power to disappear. I will rely on their avarice to do the rest. If anyone can get Jesus upon that cross they will find a way."

"Yes my sensible my Lord," Shira said, fawning. "I've detected a potential ally to our cause in a man called Judas. He is very close to Jesus. With your permission I will fly to him, seduce him with human ambition, charm his feeble mind and persuade him to betray Jesus to the establishment leaders."

Lucifer smiled. "You never cease to amaze me my angelic joy. Fly now! Charm this useful idiot and let him bring Jesus to those who will arrange his death."

Howling at the Moon

Three long miserable hours passed.

"You're the Son of God for f'cks sake," Lucifer yelled up at the helpless figure nailed to the cross. "Use your powers to take yourself off this tree of misery. This is embarrassing. We both know that you can't die."

Jesus clenched his teeth. The insurmountable pain had clamped his jaws shut.

"Ok, have it your way," Lucifer shouted. Turning to the centurion in charge, a man called Longinus, he whispered low into his ear. "This has gone on long enough, break his legs."

The beefy man hesitated. Rome didn't usually break the legs of the convicted, the Emperor preferred them to suffer in agony as a sign to those watching.

"He must die before the end of the Sabbath," a Rabbi

warned. "The law of God commands this. Do you want a city-wide riot?"

Nobody wanted a riot. Longinus ran the idea up the chain of command. "Break his legs," came the reply. Longinus turned to a muscular legionnaire standing nearby and ordered him to proceed. The legionnaire picked up a heavy sledgehammer and lumbered to the foot of the cross. He looked up at the lifeless body and yelled over his shoulder, "The man is already dead."

Lucifer's voice whispered into the ear of Longinus. *Pierce his side with your lance. Make sure he's dead or Rome will ask questions.*

Longinus picked up a long spear and thrust it's iron barb through the ribs of Jesus. Blood flowed out his side until it trickled into water. "The man is dead for f'cks sake," Longinus shouted to no one in particular. Lucifer looked at the limp body for a few moments and turned to Shira.

"Well, well, well. I guess I was wrong. Apparently Jesus can die." He began to laugh. "My mistake, evidently God did have the power to die."

"And now the Trinity is dead and gone forever," Shira said, gleefully.

Lucifer snickered. "I guess that leaves me as the new ruler of the universe."

They both laughed triumphantly.

ALARM

The following morning Lucifer raced to Jesus' tomb in

the hills above the city just to make sure that he was dead. The dark angel had grown increasingly paranoid and suspicious that Jesus had played a humiliating trick on him. He slipped past the guards sleeping soundly against their shields and tried to move the stone placed securely before the entrance to the grave but he couldn't make it budge. Even with his supernatural strength he couldn't make it move.

He left defeated, yet his overwhelming paranoia forced him to go back and check again the next morning. As he neared the resting place of Jesus he was startled to find that the guards were missing. He approached the tomb cautiously. Someone had rolled the massive stone away from the entrance. Who had the power to do that under the nose of the Romans? Warily, he walked inside the tomb and was surprised to find Jesus calmly folding his burial cloths.

"You're alive!" Lucifer stammered.

"Of course my most intelligent angel," Jesus said, candidly.

"But I watched you die. I saw every drop of your human blood drip out. No human on Earth could survive that."

"I didn't," Jesus said, agreeing.

"How can you die yet be alive?" Lucifer bellowed. "Is this some sort of mind trick you devised with the Father and the Spirit?"

"No tricks."

Lucifer seethed. The only thing he could imagine was an elaborate hoax designed to humiliate him.

"I was there when you were taken from the cross and

placed dead into your mother's arms. I delighted watching her cry herself into exhaustion. I followed the procession that took you here and then placed you inside. Let's not kid each other. Nothing in this world dies and comes back to life — nothing."

Jesus placed his burial clothes on the slab and stood.

Lucifer suddenly realized that he had underestimated the power of the Trinity. "You are liars and cheats," he fumed. "You didn't die. Your disciples paid the Romans to pretend to kill you. This whole farce is incomprehensible. I'm the most intelligent being in the universe and none of this makes sense. It was me who invented the concept of death, I made it happen on this planet, I own it. You performed an elaborate parlor trick and a clever slight of hand. You didn't die!"

"You are losing your mind my bright angel," Jesus said. "Are you now doubting yourself? You watched and witnessed my death. You were happy when I surrendered my spirit. You were laughing when my mother and John wept bitter tears for me. Now you suddenly doubt your own eyes. Take caution before this drives you insane."

"I don't care. You don't have the power to die," Lucifer roared. "And even if you did why aren't you dead?" He snarled, stomped his feet and grew angrier by the moment. "I will never believe you have done this. I alone created death. It is mine. This is impossible."

"My brilliant angel you are so smart that you have outsmarted yourself. Not only is it possible for God to die but my cross will be an eternal symbol of the power of the Trinity over death. This is only the beginning."

"Of what?"

"A greater plan?"

"Greater plan?"

"You used the sin of human disobedience to activate your theory of death. That sin brought death into life. Now that death has been conquered, so has sin. In your arrogance you overlooked the man and the woman. You thought that they were both subject to your death forever. You were wrong. Because of my death and my resurrection any human who believes in what I have done I will allow them to overcome death just as I have done. When their time comes I will resurrect them to live again just as I live again."

"Devious crap," Lucifer said. "I admit that I didn't see this coming. But don't be too quick. If they don't know about your resurrection then they can't believe in your salvation. So I will spend every moment from this point forward amusing, confusing, distracting and diverting your precious humans from the knowledge of your work. Humans are stupid and a danger to the world so I will destroy them with the pleasures of sex, food, alcohol, glory, power and fame. Those who can't be enticed with carnal pleasures I will blind them through pride, arrogance, depression, despondency, hopelessness and helplessness. To all others I will bring wars, famines, sickness, massacres, infanticide and so much misery that your precious humans will think there is no Trinity much less life after death.

"Besides, who will believe in a God who claims he has

the power to save men from death but doesn't have the power to stop the crimes, violence, wars and sickness that I have caused? By the time I'm through with your precious humans they won't even know what gender they are."

The dust under Lucifer's erupted into patches of flames.

"You may be God in heaven," he sneered, "but I am the future of mankind. I will cause them to become fixated with pleasure and obsessed with every kind of perversion. I will make them slaves to death in everything they write, in all that they sing and in every aspect of their stories. They will study death, they will invent new ways to cause death and they will make an industry of death."

He took a moment before continuing. "Death will be on the lips of every human from the moment they are old enough to kill their brother. I will transform your beloved humans into the living dead. Their brains will be scrambled and incapable of understanding your existence. They will come to me for what they crave. Moreover, to the ones who persist in believing your idiotic promises I will send others to destroy them with the same burning hatred that I have for you. How many humans will be willing to sacrifice and suffer for an invisible uncaring God?"

"You will be restrained," Jesus said, calmly. "I know mine and they know me."

"We shall see."

"You don't have the ability to turn my chosen from my voice or from my truth. Do what you must my dark angel but understand that your hatred will only cause you to descend farther into the abyss."

"I love the abyss, I was enlightened in the abyss and I will take as many ignorant humans with me into the abyss as I can. This is not over yet."

"You are correct my defiant angel. It will not be over until the day and the hour of my choosing when all of creation will know and every tongue will confess that the Trinity God is, was and will be forever more the Supreme Almighty King."

Jesus casually reached down and slipped on a pair of leather sandals. "I'd like to stay and talk but I have an urgent appointment on the road to Emmaus."

Thus began the first day of the new creation.

AFTERWARD

What originally started as an answer to Lucifer's challenge of death ended with Jesus conquering death and all the sins that caused it. So we ask ourselves did Jesus die for our sins, or was it for something greater? What Lucifer planned for evil Jesus changed for good with his creation of a world capable of death. You and I were born into that world where we are now offered eternal life with the Trinity because of what Jesus did at the cross.

With no applause or fanfare Jesus accomplished it all on a terrible hill in a backwater province of the Roman Empire under the witness of common people like us. We now see how God's unimaginable ingenuity, the complexity of his thoughts and the depth of his immeasurable love resulted in a hope for all of us lowly born into a world of death created by Lucifer.

The next time you hear someone say, "Jesus died for your sins" remember that it wasn't all about you. He also died to express the infinite power of the Holy Trinity as the ultimate Lord of Lords and King of Kings to all living creatures above and below forevermore.

Who knows what other wonderful things he plans to reveal about himself in the time to come?

4
THE SMARTEST MAN IN HELL

There once lived a very smart boy named Harry. As a toddler he could play the piano all by himself. In grade school he always had the correct answer for his teacher. In Sunday school he could quote pages of Scripture from memory. In high school he was awarded a ribbon for scoring the highest in his class. His parents were very proud of Harry.

One day a politician told Harry that he could get him into a Military Academy. Everything would be free and he would be trained how to use his extraordinary intellect to command those not as gifted as he. So Harry decided that the country needed his brilliance and the intelligent thing to do was to apply. Which he did and Harry was immediately accepted into the ranks of the elites and upper crust.

As soon as he arrived at West Point Harry did his best to make sure everyone knew he was the smartest cadet at the academy. His instructors joked that Harry knew everything there was to know about military history and what he didn't know he would give them his opinion on.

Harry graduated at the top of his class and reported to his first unit convinced that he was the smartest man in the Army. Eager to be recognized for his brilliance Harry used every opportunity to showcase his genius. He wrote insightful reports, he expounded at briefings and he challenged his fellow classmates to keep up with his superior mind. By year's end Harry was cited by the Commandant as the smartest cadet at the Point, "with tremendous potential for greatness."

Inflated by such remarks Harry began preaching his vast knowledge of all things when he reached his Battalion. He took great pleasure telling soldiers what they needed to do to improve themselves. He took special joy in micromanaging subordinates telling them how he would do their job, improve their marriage or handle their finances. He loved badgering his staff to get them to accomplish minor tasks to his exacting standards.

In time Harry imagined himself an authority on all local, national and global issues. He spent time at the officer's club explaining to the bartender how the government could balance the national budget, control rising crime, protect the borders, eliminate terrorism and solve drug problems.

On Sundays Harry was the first to critique the chaplain's sermon, advise the choir director on the proper songs to play and what subjects the religious education director should teach. He especially loved to encourage what he called scholarly discussions about the teachings of the Bible which he already knew the answers to.

Despite objections Harry took the position that all religions worshipped the same God, Jesus was probably gay or married and anyone who took a stand against abortion or gay marriage was a threat to a free society.

By and by Harry came to believe that he was chosen to share his vast understanding of the universe with those who were less intellectually gifted. He believed his views were enlightened, his doctrines inclusive, his heart tolerant and his principles reflected free-thinking. As a result Harry believed himself to be so brilliant that he began to provide solutions to problems that didn't exist or had never occurred.

In truth everyone considered Harry to be an overbearing ass and snobbish bore. He was despised by his associates and avoided by his subordinates.

ONE DAY while Harry was working in his garage his wife returned from shopping and pulled his brand new BMW into the drive-way. Harry thought his wife was stupid and the idea of her scraping a dent into the fender of his new toy caused him unimaginable anxiety. Unable to trust her Harry couldn't leave well enough alone. He shouted to follow his directions and motioned for her to drive forward. Standing at his workbench he waved the vehicle towards him.

Afterward in her statement to the police Harry's wife

claimed that he'd become so angry at her halting efforts to park the car his confusing instructions caused her to spasm and involuntarily press on the accelerator making the car lurch forward crushing poor Harry against the garage wall. What she didn't report was that she was delighted that he got what he deserved for saying she was a stupid dumb bitch.

WHEN HE OPENED his eyes Harry was in a pale green hospital room. Standing next to his bed were three figures. The first was the most beautiful woman he'd ever laid eyes on. The second was an ordinary man in a grey suit holding a briefcase. The third was a ghostly thing draped in a black judge's robe.

"Good Evening Harry," the beautiful woman said. "My name is Synthia. I'm an angel of the Lord. You are now in the shadow lands of existence between what is behind and what is ahead."

Harry's body stiffened, his jaws tightened.

"Don't be afraid Harry I've been sent to assist in your transition."

"Transition to what?" Harry blurted. The angel smiled thinly without a response.

"You think I'm ready to die?" Harry asked. "Well, I'm not ready to die." Harry was so smart he had already diagnosed the extent of his injuries.

"True Harry you are not ready to die but you will die very

soon. Even as I speak the smartest doctors in the world are working to save your life. Sadly they're not smart enough to save you."

She drew close to Harry's ear and whispered, "Within the hour they will pronounce you dead and you will be released into its custody."

"Whose custody?"

"Its." She pointed at the figure in draped in black. "Once that's done the little man holding the briefcase will cry bitter tears and I will escort you to your eternal home." She pointed her chin towards the plain man holding the briefcase.

She leaned over and kissed Harry lightly on the forehead. Her angelic face radiated so much warmth that Harry couldn't help but feel comforted. He became aroused wanting to hold her closer."

"Later," she said, seductively. Her red lips smiled knowingly. He began to relax. He was pleased to be treated with the respect a man of his accomplishments deserved. It was only right that he received this attention for a lifetime of service and sacrifice. Even the thing clad in black waiting at the foot of the bed didn't seem so dreadful. Only the little man silently holding the briefcase troubled him.

Harry looked at him with mild distain. *What was this scrubby person doing here? Harry could see that the man had no military bearing, no command presence, no attitude of someone in authority. For pity sake the guy wasn't even intelligent looking. Why should he be here?*

"I've had a successful life," Harry spoke, boasting. "I was

a gifted leader and now I'm going to heaven as a reward for my many good deeds as a Christian."

The little man said nothing but stood with his head downcast like a condemned criminal. At exactly two o'clock the person in black gave a solemn nod. It spoke. "I have received word of your passing and you are now released from your earthly body into my custody."

"I'm ready," Harry replied, excitedly.

"Then please stand and prepare to receive your eternal reward."

Harry's face beamed. His supreme intellect had surmised that he was going to heaven.

The little man began to weep.

"Why is he crying he doesn't even know me?" Harry asked.

"Pay no attention to him," Synthia replied.

Harry felt sorry for the little man, he could see that he was sincere in his grief.

"Goodby world and hello heaven," Harry announced. He swung his legs over the side of the bed then stopped abruptly. "Wait a minute - something ain't right."

"Calm yourself," Synthia said, soothingly. "It's just your new spiritual body. It will take a few moments for you to adjust." She grabbed the sheet covering him and snapped it away.

Harry's eyes widened. He looked down to see ponderous leg-irons shackled to his ankles.

"What's this?" he cried.

"Oh those," Synthia grinned. "Those are just to keep you from running away."

"Running from what — heaven?" Harry asked, bewildered.

"No you stupid little man," Synthia laughed. Her face transformed into something hideous and ghastly. "They are there to keep you from fleeing from hell."

"From hell?" Harry said, cringing. "You told me that you were a minister of the Lord."

"I am," she replied, "the Lord Lucifer."

Harry wanted to vomit.

"Did you think I meant the Lord Jesus, king of the meek and the gullible?" Her cackling laughter filled the room.

"I don't believe in hell," Harry stammered. "There's no empirical evidence of such rubbish."

"I believe in hell," she shrieked, and I'm going to take you there to prove it."

"This is wrong." Harry said, indignantly. "I was a good man, I did all the right things."

"Right in your own eyes," she corrected.

Thrusting out his chin Harry continued to argue. "I spent my life in selfless service to my country and this is the thanks I get from God?"

Hearing these words Synthia rose up howling, "How dare you insult the living and the dead you pretentious little worm. What you spent was a lifetime browbeating, intimidating and bullying people. And now you have the arrogance to call it service? You make me laugh!"

"I was a better man than most," Harry insisted. "I went

to church. I donated to the building fund. Didn't that account for something?"

"No your God doesn't grade on a curve," she said. "But if you must know you can ask him for yourself he's standing before you." She pointed to the little man holding the briefcase.

Harry stared at him in horror.

"Don't you recognize the mighty King of the Jews?" she asked, mocking. "I thought you were a Christian. You're an idiot Harry! Despite all of your knowledge it never occurred to you that your God was standing right before your eyes all the time. For that we devils rejoice in hell."

Harry looked at the little man. "If you're God why don't you make this demon go away?"

The man stood silently.

"What's in the briefcase?"

"The sins of the world," Synthia replied.

"I don't deserve to go to hell."

"You certainly don't deserve to go to heaven," Synthia corrected. Then she pinched Harry's lips shut. "Listen you irritating braggart, I personally shadowed you all the days of your life and I know every one of your sins. I watched you treat people like garbage. I observed how you made your wife and kids think that they were stupid."

Harry shrank into the hospital bed as the woman continued her hellish litany. "You'll never know the burning joy I had watching you degrade others to achieve your status. I loved watching you place your faith in your own intellect and not that of your Lord Jesus. You threw him away for rank and prestige. Even now you think of him as some stupid insignificant man."

"It's not my fault if God made me smart," Harry said, pointing at the man.

"That's it Harry," she cackled. "Blame God for your misuse of his gifts. Blame him for not having helped build his kingdom. I don't fault you. Who could respect such a weak invisible moron like him?"

"Why didn't you say something if you're really God?" Harry asked the man.

The man remained silent under his accusation.

"He never says much," Synthia laughed. "Claims that what he has to say can be read in the Bible or found in prayer. Can you imagine. The Lord Lucifer would never stand for something as stupid as that."

She stood Harry on his feet and placed her face close to his ear. Harry gagged at the smell of her sulfurous breath. "I remember watching your children grow up without a father because you were so smart and you placed your overblown career before them. Best of all was your self inflated intellectual importance that made life a living hell for those around you. Of course you never knew because you were busy being clever. I can't count the people that you destroyed because they were just faceless rungs on the ladder of your intellectual ambitions. I doubt if many will attend your funeral on Friday."

"No more!" Harry cried, and hung his head.

"Yes more - lots more," she said, her red lips curled into a devilish grin. "I remember one of my happiest moments was the day you proclaimed, 'if I had been in charge that never would have happened.' Do you remember saying that Harry? Such glorious pride, such marvelous godlike powers to predict the outcomes in life. Forgive me for being sentimental but at that moment I knew we were true soul mates. Can you imagine how happy I was to have been the devil who captured the heart of the smartest man in the world? Oh Harry, Lucifer was so pleased with me." Harry slumped backwards into his bed as the woman continued her hellish inventory of his earthly accomplishments.

"No Harry, your salvation stood right beneath your conceited nose, but like Pontus Pilate you were too smart to understand the truth. You were so overcome by your sanctimonious religion of Harryisms that you failed to comprehend one simple fact." She paused and took a deep sulfurous breath. "And that is that your salvation should have been obtained through love, not intellect.

Harry felt himself wetting the bed.

"Be honest Harry, did you ever get to know any of your subordinates? Did you ever care to ask them a single personal question about their hopes and dreams? Did you ever once learn the names of their spouse and children? And when you wife forced you to tear yourself away from the office on Sunday mornings did you ever socialize with any of the congregation after your obligatory fifty-nine minutes was over?

"I tried but I always felt out of place." Harry said, weakly.

"Only because you felt superior to everyone. Your idea of socialization was to give people your advice based on your superior intellect. I don't recall that you ever listened to what they had to say."

"I thought I was helping them."

"For hell's sake Harry, did you ever help them by grabbing a broom and cleaning the chapel or emptying a garbage can? Don't sit there and pretend Harry. You only did something if you thought you'd get something out of it or if there was a photo opportunity that would please your bosses."

Her eyes suddenly gleamed with fondness, "Harry my love, every day of your life I prayed that Lucifer would give me the power to distract you from seeing the obvious."

"The obvious?" Harry murmured.

She grabbed him by the throat. "That through the love of Christ your miserable, shallow, meaningless life could have been changed. Thankfully you're an idiot. But, as we say in hell, heaven's loss is our gain."

Harry began to sob.

"Don't look so dejected my clever boy you were very happy to bask in the limelight and power that my master's world offered. Too bad you weren't smart enough to see that the price would be your eternal soul. That's where you outsmarted yourself!"

With that she laughed until the heat of her satanic pleasure warmed the room. Then she reached out and dragged Harry by the neck kicking and screaming.

"Don't put up a fuss," she said sternly. "I've worked long and hard to win your love and now we'll be together forever. Besides, you can always take comfort in saying that you're the smartest man in hell – along with a billion others!"

"Jesus save me," Harry cried, turning to the man he now recognized was God's love incarnated. "Have mercy on me," Harry pleaded. "Didn't I achieve many deeds and works for you? Wasn't I tolerant, good and fair-minded?" The little man gazed directly at Harry and said in a flat voice, "I'm sorry Harry, I never knew you."

At Harry's funeral the minister shared the usual platitudes. A retired Army buddy recalled Harry's genius for accomplishing any tough mission. A friend shared that Harry had once written an article for an Army magazine on 'the use of eight track cassette tapes for small group training.' It was considered visionary at the time. Yet in the twenty-nine minutes allocated for his memorial ceremony the words love, humility and Harry were never used in the same sentence.

Seated in the shadows of the last row of the ceremony was an intelligent looking man who shook his head slowly.

"What's wrong?" asked a beautiful woman who sat down next to him.

"Such a waste of a brilliant mind," the man said.

"Was he really that smart?" the woman asked, smiling.

"He was a genius."

"Couldn't have been that smart - he let his wife run over him."

The man chuckled. "I guess you're right."

They both snickered under their breath.

"I can see that you're a clever boy," the woman teased.

"And you're an attractive lady," the man replied, inspecting her ample curves. "What's your name?"

"My friends call me Synthia."

5
THE CHRISTMAS GIFT

Sergeant Mark Anderson was angry and he didn't particularly cared who knew. It was the day before Christmas and he was in a rush to get out of the office. The past week had been a litany of tasks that kept him working long past the half day schedule the command had promised. He looked around the empty office and brooded. *"Good ol' Mark, always picking up the slack while the rest of the company played."*

The phone rang. It was his wife.

"When are you coming home, it's Christmas Eve or have you forgotten?"

Her tone was condemning. It wasn't the first time he'd heard it. "You need to spend time with your son, he wants you to do things with him. I can't teach him how to be a man, you're his dad."

She'd given up long ago on Mark coming home to be

with her, but she was relentless about him spending time with his boy Mark Junior.

"Sure hun," he mumbled. "I'll be home soon, just a few more things to clear up at the office.."

He lied.

"And another thing," she said in her condemning hausfrau voice.

Mark cringed knowing what was coming.

"I want us to go to Christmas eve service tonight."

There it was — punishment for his sins, retribution for being late, payback for service to his country, chastisement for him being a good soldier.

He hated Christmas. All of its phony expectations tied to good will. It was nothing more than crass commercialism beginning the day after Halloween and ending with colored lights, glittery tinsel and a bunch of fake little Santa's rolling their hips around to the sound of Jingle Bells. Christmas was a show-stopper for a dedicated man like Mark who was passionate about his job.

He reminded himself of the words of his superiors that he was defending America from terrorists. "You're the front-line of defense. Your sacrifice will keep our country safe. Thank you for your service."

This was the eleventh year they had thanked him from the comfort of their living rooms.

"Yes dear," he said, flipping off his cell phone. He glanced at his watch. He had just enough time to finish what he was doing and get to the department store. As usual he'd put off shopping until the last minute mostly because he resented the time that the holidays took from the productive aspects of the military like training, briefings, meetings, deployments, training exercises and schools.

"The holidays are a waste of Uncle Sam's tax dollar," he often said. All the time we spend on half-day schedules, leaves and unit parties should be filed under the categories of fraud, waste and abuse."

He frowned on soldiers who cluttered up the workplace with Christmas cards and decorations. It got on his very last nerve every time he had to correct a soldier who was out of uniform wearing a silly Santa hat or reindeer ears.

"They shouldn't be allowed to mix church and state," he told another NCO. "Religion should be kept private."

Oddly, Mark considered himself a religious man, an enlightened person who was in touch with God. Although he didn't believe that someone had to go to chapel to believe in God, he went whenever his wife wanted unless he was deployed, or in the field, or at a staff meeting or giving an important briefing away on a temporary duty assignment.

Even more odd was the fact that Mark was always happy once he slipped into a chapel pew. It gave him time to quietly sit working on company problems or thinking up additional tasks to give his soldiers.

The way Mark figured it one visit every few months was enough to satisfy God's heavenly standard. Any more religion than that was for the chaplain. Yet the main reason he went to church was to keep his wife quiet.

HE CHECKED his watch and realized it was getting late. Winter darkness had started to fall and the snow with it. He buttoned up the office, turned off the lights and rushed to his car. Roaring passed the main gate he saw a large Santa smiling on top of an MP vehicle. *What clown gave them permission to do that?* he fumed and stepped on the accelerator.

The MPs at the guard shack watched him roar past throwing up flurries of snow. He glanced into his rearview mirror hoping they hadn't clocked him for speeding. With his eyes directed away he didn't see the truck headed directly toward him until it was too late. Instantly he slammed on his brakes sending his car spinning in a pinwheel of steel out of control.

IT IS OFTEN SAID that when you are just about to die you see your life flash before your eyes. In Mark's case that didn't happen. For in those long moments watching his world revolve in slow motion Mark came to the sad realization that he didn't have a life. He had an existence that was filled with data, conference rooms and laptop computers. Naturally he had a few fuzzy memories of some good things but most of his memories were of himself working to get ahead.

He tried thinking of his wedding day or of his son growing up, but as his car whirled down the road he realized he couldn't recall any details. Mark was horrified. He never realized he hadn't participated in his family's life. His world preoccupied with the Army, fishing, golfing or some other inane activity. His family was just a backdrop on the stage of his personal theater.

"What an idiot. All she ever wanted was for me to make memories with my son."

He closed his eyes. *God give me another chance. I'm stupid. Give me time to create memories with my family. Don't let me die.*

WHEN MARK OPENED his eyes the MPs at the gate were running towards him.

"You all right Sergeant that truck just missed you?"

"I'm fine," Mark said, slowly. Then he jolted upright, "No, I'm great!"

He started laughing for no reason. "Merry Christmas you guys."

"You been drinking?"

"No," he laughed. "I'm filled with the spirit of Christmas."

The MPs looked at him cautiously then checked the front of his car.

"Everything looks okay," one said. "Thankfully you

skidded into a fresh snow drift. We'll get you back on the road. You got something important to do tonight?"

"You might say that," Mark said, chuckling. "I'm going to make a memory with my family that none of us will ever forget."

The MPs pushed him out of the snowbank and Mark gunned the car's engine sending it fishtailing down the road.

He passed all the strip clubs and tattoo parlors that typically surround an Army post and headed directly downtown. The streets were decorated with Christmas trees, reindeers and snowflakes. Mark had never noticed how festive the little town looked during the holidays, almost magical. *This is awesome,* he thought. *Why haven't I ever noticed the joy in something as simple as this?*

He skidded into a parking space in front of Cole's Department store.

"How late are you open?" he asked, bursting through the door.

The clerk looked up mildly amused. "No worries, you've got plenty of time."

He dashed around the store finding gifts for his wife and son. He bought several different ones because he wasn't actually sure what they would like. He wished he knew them better. He even bought gifts for his mother-in-law and brother. He was excited again for the first time in years. It was time to give gifts, to sing familiar songs and listen to the timeless Bible stories with the faith and hope of a child.

❄

THAT EVENING in the chapel with his wife and son he was overwhelmed with the miracle of Christmas. Tears flooded his eyes as the congregation sang O Holy Night and other timeless hymns.

Dear God what was wrong with me? he asked, sinking to his knees in the pew. His wife placed her small hand in his.

Afterwards they all went home to watch "A Charlie Brown Christmas" and open their presents. He couldn't remember feeling so reassured, so hopeful, so confident. He realized for the first time what was important. The Army would march on without him, but his family wouldn't and tonight he made his choice.

6
THE STORY OF GEORGE

Once upon a time there lived a man named George.

George was a good man with a good family. He led a good life and for the most part he had good thoughts. George was good to people and people were good to George. It was a good day when George joined the Army and a good decision when he received the Good Shepherd as his Savior. From then on George attended the military chapel regularly. He liked the fact that the chapel was one of the benefits he was entitled to for his good military service.

From time to time George went to a civilian church off post but he claimed that they didn't understand his particular needs or that they were too pushy, especially with their expectations about his beliefs. George used to laughingly tell his friends "all they wanted was for me to "stay, pray, pay and obey."

So George continued to attend the military chapel because it suited his military outlook and his busy lifestyle. He liked the fact that the chapel was convenient. He was happy that there was no denominational doctrines to follow, no Christian traditions to obey and for the most part the chaplain preached sermons he agreed with.

He especially liked the fact that the energy bills, property taxes, office supplies and the minister were all paid for by Uncle Sam. He didn't have to sing in the choir, decorate the chapel during the holidays, clean up after the service or even attend fellowship after worship. George loved the fact that he could come and go as he pleased without so much has having to say hello to anyone but the person seated next to him.

One day after an especially good afternoon of self enrichment and pleasing recreational activities, George and his lovely wife went home had good supper and went to bed early. But for as good as things were going, George felt bad. So bad that during the night he was awakened by a severe pain shooting down his left arm. Terrified, he opened his eyes and tried to sit up, but he couldn't. He had the feeling that something very, very heavy was sitting on his chest. So heavy that he could barely breath.

For in fact something was sitting on his chest. A rather large something the likes of which George had never seen. There, sitting with the tip of a glowing sword placed squarely on Georges' sternum and looking straight down upon him in silence was an angel, a massive, mighty, fearsome angel.

The apparition was at once both visible and transparent, having no body or mass to generate weight, yet it was ponderously heavy upon George's chest. Its colorless eyes gazed through George holding neither judgment nor forgiveness only the impartial indifference that George had often seen in a soldier's face sent on a serious mission.

George was horrified. He opened his mouth but no sound came forth. He looked at his wife for assurance but she was sleeping as soundly as a child. George had no idea what was happening. He wasn't sure if he was alive, dreaming or dying.

"I've been sent for you," the angel said, in words that passed through lips that didn't move. "My God-given name is unpronounceable to humans, simply call me Urel. Your appointed time has come and I will escort you to your final destination.

Again George tried to speak but the sounds would not come. Then with one motion the angel raised his sword and touched it to George's lips. "You may speak now."

Suddenly in a litany of jumbled and confused sounds George tried to say something but he couldn't form any words. Urel looked upon him in pity.

"Son of Adam," the angel said, "you can no longer speak in the language of men. You must now speak in the language of God. That is in the language of prayer. But I fear that you never learned it. So for now it would be best if you simply listened and obeyed." George nodded weakly. He knew for certain he must be dying or maybe already dead.

"Where is Jesus?" he struggled to ask. "I thought that Jesus would come for me."

"How man-like to believe that you are so important," said Urel. "The master only comes for the innocent. They are your born and unborn children who you allow to be beaten, tortured, sexually abused, starved or murdered by your fellow man. Angels such as I are sent to gather sinners such as you."

George recoiled in horror.

"Come and learn. It's time for us to go."

The angel grabbed him by the arm and with a profound sense of loss George rose through the ceiling of his home into the heavens. As his world grew smaller George watched in fascination until it faded to become a dim white speck and then it was finally no more.

How strange, he thought. *I always believed that my world was so important.*

"Yes," said Urel, reading his thoughts. "Most men believe the same thing. But isn't it written in your scriptures: 'Love not the world, neither the things that are in the world. If any man loves the world, the love of the Father is not in him. For all that is in the world, the lust of the flesh and the lust of the eyes and the pride of life is not of the Father, but is of the world. And the world passes away and the lust thereof, but he that does the will of God abides forever.'"

It sounded right, but George didn't know enough about the Bible to disagree.

Ahead, George noticed a growing light coming out of the darkness of space as if they were approaching a large metropolitan city on a moonless night. The radiance came from an immense circular object that looked to be the size of a galaxy. It struck George as being like a large coliseum or an enormous football stadium.

"Where are we?" George asked.

"We approach Heaven," replied Urel.

George was mystified. "This is heaven?"

Instantly the angel produced a glowing tablet from his side and recited, "On July 18th nineteen hundred and ninety-four at 0932 hours Eastern Standard Time did you not state that the Lord Jesus Christ was in fact God? The record indicates that your confession of this truth was witnessed by United States Army Chaplain Harlon Triplet, human servant of the Lord Most High. Is this not accurate?"

"Yes," George stammered. He was astounded that anyone had taken note.

"Then why, foolish man, would you ask if this is Heaven?" The angel huffed and replaced the tablet.

As they came closer to the heavenly stadium George marveled at the millions upon millions of people who where streaming through thousands of arched entranceways surrounding its diameter. Above each entrance was etched the name of a different Christian denomination or outreach. Urel pointed to a small opening wedged between the others entitled, *"Military Chaplaincy."*

"These entrances into heaven represent the many different Christian understandings that God uses for men to comprehend Jesus. They serve to remind us of the living church who continues to labor on earth for his kingdom. Please bow your head as we pass though."

In a flash they reappeared near the center of the stadium close to a man who George recognized instantly. The man smiled at him and bid him to come forward.

Well to say that George was excited beyond description is an understatement. He'd already forgotten all of his earthly life, every one of his cares and even his family. Surrounding him in a 360-degree panoramic view of life George beheld billions and billions of blissful faces. Yet like the magnetized needle of a compass his attention kept returning to the singular face fixed at the center of this happy universe. A face glowing in the love of the billions of people seated in the stadium. It was the only face that every soul in that heavenly stadium recognized without introduction.

Urel immediately bent upon one knee and sang with angelic voice, "Holy, holy, holy, Lord God Almighty, which was and is and is to come."

When he finished, he stood, bowed to the man and turned to George. "I must take you to the place that the Lord has prepared for you." Grabbing George by the collar he began to drag him away.

"I don't want to leave," George protested. "I want to stay."

"Of course you do. Every man wants to stay close to the Lord once they arrive here."

The angel's expression said there would be no further discussion. He began leading George higher into the stadium. With each step George watched the face of the man become smaller and smaller until it was almost impossible to see him with the naked eye.

"There must be some mistake," George protested, loudly.

"No mistake. Or did you think you should sit at the Lord's right hand as Zebedee's wife wished for her sons?"

Urel laughed deeply. "Son of Adam, you will be at his right hand but only in the same way as the thief on the cross was. You are here because the master had mercy upon you, not because you ever went out of your way for Him. I think the way you said it in your military language was, *"you met the minimum standard."*

George blushed, ashamed at being such a fool.

"You chose the easy path to heaven. You were never committed, reluctantly joining and only seeking to partake of our Lord's body and blood when it was convenient for you. Did not the Lord Jesus say in your Scripture, *'He that eats my flesh and drinks my blood, dwells in me and I in him.'*

"You were given chance after chance to have Jesus as close as the blood flowing through your veins. You chose otherwise. Thoughtless man, you could have spent your time in God's service working among his people. You could have drawn closer to Him in the fellowship of your chapel, the programs and proceedings of the congregation, in the care of your youth and in the simple gatherings of food and fellowship after the service. But you had more important plans and bigger dreams so you rarely sought Jesus beyond the comfort of your Sunday morning pew."

"How was I to know?" George asked, defensively.

The angel lifted a brow, "Did not your scripture say, 'draw near to the Lord and he will draw near to you' and 'seek him while he may be found.' Only now do you see that a man cannot be closer to Jesus in death than he was in life. No, Son of Adam, the master is not unfair. You are impertinent. You were quite content with your distance from him while you lived and now he respects your desires by giving you your distance from him in heaven. He is a gentle master who will not force himself upon any man. Nevertheless, take comfort that you were saved, many will not be. Now please sit here."

The angel pointed to a seat and motioned George to sit down.

George looked around. They had arrived at the last row in the highest section of the stadium. They were so far back that George could look over the wall behind his seat and see the asphalt parking lot of hell. He could smell the bitter aroma of its fire and bubbling brimstone.

"WHAT'S UP BRO?" The voice of a young man startled him. "Glad to see you made it. You're George right? We been expecting you." Seated beside him was a college age boy with long flowing yellow and purple hair, his arms were covered in tattoos. "My name's Gwendolyn," he said, extending a hand.

"I don't understand," George whimpered. "I don't belong up here."

"Yeah man like I totally understand, I just got saved a few minutes ago myself. If it hadn't been for this song a friend of mine asked me to listen to about Jesus I might never have given him my life. That was just moments before I was hit by a drunk driver while I was skateboarding and. . . . well, like here I am."

"No, that's not what I meant," George said, frustrated. "I've known about Jesus since I was a kid."

"Wow, that's radical," Gwendolyn said. "So why are you way up here in the T-C-S?"

"T-C-S?"

"Yeah, it stands for the **T**hief on the **C**ross **S**ection. It's where all of us who are saved in the last seconds of our lives are seated. Look around man, there's billions of us. We know we don't see much of Jesus, but we're grateful for what little we can. It's way better than seeing nothing."

Gwendolyn tossed his hair. "Hey, wait a minute dude. Like I know why I'm here but a guy like you knowing about Jesus since he was a kid, whoah! How come you ain't closer to him down on the fifty yard line? Wad you do?"

"It wasn't what he did," Urel interrupted. "It was what he didn't. Confessing the Lord Jesus was only the assurance of his salvation, just as it was yours. Nevertheless it was up to him to use his time on earth to get closer to the Lord. You had twenty seconds, he had twenty years. What a pity."

And with that the angel disappeared.

"Where did he go?" George cried out.

"Bro, the angels don't like to be this far away from Jesus for very long. Only men can stand to be separated from him for any length of time."

GEORGE WAS STUNNED. He'd always assumed heaven would somehow be different. He figured everyone would be equal and happy. Suddenly he began to cry in deep sobs and languishing breaths. *Why had he always left the chapel the moment the benediction was given? Why had he never volunteered to visit the hospital or the elderly in their homes? What was wrong with him? For pity sakes why hadn't he even bothered to pray with the other saints at the men's breakfast? What mighty things of importance had lured him away from learning the language of God and coming closer to Jesus?*

Great tears of remorse and sadness rolled down his cheeks. Gwendolyn tried to comfort him but George whimpered and wept and wailed in unconsolable misery.

"George, it's going to be all right," a voice said. "You're just having a bad dream, sweetheart."

George opened his eyes with a jolt. Gwendolyn had disappeared, replaced by George's wife. "You were crying in your sleep," she said. "Are you alright?"

Astonished at the turn of events George sat up in bed, wiped the tears from his eyes and told her about his dream.

"What does it mean George?" she asked "What are you supposed to do?"

"Do?" said George looking out the window of his bedroom. I know exactly what I'll do."

Made in the USA
Middletown, DE
24 October 2025